"What was that?"

DJ began brushing the snow off her backside.

"A kiss. Apparently it's been a while for you, as well," Beau said. He began helping her brush off the snow.

"I can do it myself," she snapped. She wanted to tell him that she'd only kissed him back because he'd taken her by surprise. But he didn't give her a chance to lie.

"Don't look so shocked. It was just a kiss, right? It wasn't like either of us felt anything."

"I was asking why you thought you could get away with kissing me like that. Or was that part of the bargain you made with my father?" She hoped he caught the sarcasm.

"I was merely doing my job protecting you. Since the one thing your father didn't make clear is who I'm protecting you from. As for the kiss, it just seemed like a good idea. It won't happen again."

"You're right about that, because I don't need your so-called protection."

CARDWELL CHRISTMAS CRIME SCENE

New York Times Bestselling Author

B.J. DANIELS

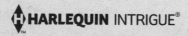
HARLEQUIN INTRIGUE®

With utmost appreciation I dedicate this Cardwell book to Kimberly Rocha, the craziest, most loving, generous, truly beautiful fan I've yet to meet.

Recycling programs for this product may not exist in your area.

ISBN-13: 978-0-373-69944-5

Cardwell Christmas Crime Scene

Copyright © 2016 by Barbara Heinlein

Printed in U.S.A.

HARLEQUIN®
www.Harlequin.com

B.J. Daniels is a *New York Times* and *USA TODAY* bestselling author. She wrote her first book after a career as an award-winning newspaper journalist and author of thirty-seven published short stories. She lives in Montana with her husband, Parker, and three springer spaniels. When not writing, she quilts, boats and plays tennis. Contact her at bjdaniels.com, on Facebook or on Twitter, @bjdanielsauthor.

Books by B.J. Daniels

Harlequin Intrigue

Cardwell Cousins

Rescue at Cardwell Ranch
Wedding at Cardwell Ranch
Deliverance at Cardwell Ranch
Reunion at Cardwell Ranch

Crime Scene at Cardwell Ranch
Justice at Cardwell Ranch
Cardwell Ranch Trespasser
Christmas at Cardwell Ranch
Cardwell Christmas Crime Scene

HQN Books

The Montana Hamiltons

Wild Horses
Lone Rider
Lucky Shot
Hard Rain

Visit the Author Profile page at Harlequin.com for more titles.

CAST OF CHARACTERS

***Beau Tanner*—**The cowboy private investigator made a promise years ago, and he never goes back on his promises.

***Dee Anna Justice*—**DJ's life began to unravel the moment she realized someone had been in her apartment—and left her a "present"...

***Marietta Pisani*—**She would do anything to protect her family.

***Carlotta Pisani Justice Gianni*—**Her deathbed confession changed everything.

***Roger Douglas*—**The attorney had his own reasons for wanting the Pisani legacy upheld.

***Ester Brown*—**The loyal housekeeper couldn't keep the family secrets any longer.

***Walter Justice*—**He kept the truth from his daughter to protect her from the family she knew nothing about.

***Zinnia Jameson*—**She lost the love of her life when Walter married someone else.

Chapter One

DJ Justice opened the door to her apartment and froze. Nothing looked out of place and yet she took a step back. Her gaze went to the lock. There were scratches around the keyhole. The lock set was one of the first things she'd replaced when she'd rented the apartment.

She eased her hand into the large leather hobo bag that she always carried. Her palm fit smoothly around the grip of the weapon, loaded and ready to fire, as she slowly pushed open the door.

The apartment was small and sparsely furnished. She never stayed anywhere long, so she collected nothing of value that couldn't fit into one suitcase. Spending years on the run as a child, she'd had to leave places in the middle of the night with only minutes to pack.

But that had changed over the past few years. She'd just begun to feel…safe. She liked her job, felt content here. She should have known it couldn't last.

The door creaked open wider at the touch of her finger, and she quickly scanned the living area. Moving deeper into the apartment, she stepped to the open bathroom door and glanced in. Nothing amiss. At a glance she could see the bathtub, sink and toilet as well as the mirror on the medicine cabinet. The shower door was clear glass. Nothing behind it.

That left just the bedroom. As she stepped soundlessly toward it, she wanted to be wrong. And yet she knew someone had been here. But why break in unless he or she planned to take something?

Or leave something?

Like the time she'd found the bloody hatchet on the fire escape right outside her window when she was eleven. That message had been for her father, the blood from a chicken, he'd told her. Or maybe it hadn't even been blood, he'd said. As if she hadn't seen his fear. As if they hadn't thrown everything they owned into suitcases and escaped in the middle of the night.

She moved to the open bedroom door. The room was small enough that there was sufficient room only for a bed and a simple nightstand with one shelf. The book she'd been reading the night before was on the nightstand, nothing else.

The double bed was made—just as she'd left it.

She started to turn away when she caught a glimmer of something out of the corner of her eye. Ice ran down her spine as she dropped the gun back into her shoulder bag and stepped closer. Something had been tucked between the pillows and duvet. Gingerly picking up the edge of the duvet, she peeled it back an inch at a time. DJ braced herself for something bloody and dismembered, her mind a hamster on a wheel, spinning wildly.

But what she found was more disturbing than blood and guts. As she uncovered part of it, she saw familiar blank eyes staring up at her. Her breath caught in her throat as tears stung her eyes.

"Trixie?" she whispered, voice breaking, as she stared at the small rag doll's familiar face.

On the run with her father, she'd had little more than the clothes on her back except for the rag doll that had been her only companion since early childhood.

"We should throw this old thing away," her father had said after a dog tore the doll from her hands once and he'd had to chase it down to retrieve what was left because she'd been so hysterical. "I'll buy you another doll. A pretty one, not some stuffed fabric one," he'd pleaded.

She'd been so upset that he'd relented and let her keep the doll she'd always known as Trixie. But she could tell that he would have been happier to get rid of the thing. She wondered if it brought him bad memories, since it was clear that the doll was handmade. Even the clothing. She liked to pretend that her mother had made it for her. If her mother hadn't died in childbirth.

Was that why her father wished she didn't care so much for the doll? Because it brought back the grief, the loss? That might explain why he had seemed to want nothing to do with anything from the past, including her doll. Not that she'd ever understood her father. .

Life with him had been sparse and sporadic. He had somehow kept her fed and clothed and managed to get her into school—at least for a while until they were uprooted again. But the incident with the doll now made her wonder.

From as far back as she could remember, she'd believed that the doll with the sewn face and the dull, dark stitched eyes needed her as much as she needed it.

Now she half feared all she would find was Trixie's dismembered head. But as she drew back the covers, she saw that the body was still intact. Someone had left it for her tucked under the covers almost…tenderly. With trembling fingers, she picked up the treasured rag doll, afraid something awful had been done to her that would spoil one of the few good memories she had of her childhood.

Cupping the precious doll in her hands, DJ began to cry—for herself and for Trixie. The doll was in incredible shape for how old she was, not to mention what she must have been through over the years. DJ thought of her being lost, someone discarding her in a trash can as nothing more than junk and that awful feeling she'd had that she would never see her again.

So how had Trixie miraculously turned up again?

Heart in her throat, she looked closer at the doll.

Something was wrong.

The doll looked exactly like Trixie, but... She studied the handmade clothing. It looked as pristine as the doll. Maybe whoever had found it had washed it, taken care of it all these years...

For what possible purpose?

As happy as she'd been to see the doll again, now she realized how unlikely that was. Why would any-one care about some silly rag doll? And how could someone possibly know she was the one who'd lost it all those years ago?

After being her constant companion from as far back as she could remember, Trixie had been the worse for wear before DJ had misplaced her. The doll had spent too many years tucked under one of DJ's chubby arms. So how—

With a jolt, she recalled the accident she'd had with the doll and the dog that had taken off with it all those years ago. The dog had ripped off one of Trixie's legs. With DJ screaming for help, her father had chased down the dog, retrieved the leg and later, at her pleading, painstakingly sewn it back on with the only thread he could find, black.

Her fingers trembling, she lifted the dress hem and peered under the only slightly faded red pantaloons. With both shock and regret, she saw that there was no black thread. No seam where the leg had been reattached.

This wasn't her doll.

It surprised her that at thirty-five, she could feel such loss for something she'd been missing for so many years.

She stared at the rag doll, now more confused than ever. Why would people break into her apartment to leave it for her? They had to have known that she'd owned one exactly like it. Wouldn't they realize that she'd know the difference between hers and this one? Or was that the point?

DJ studied the doll more closely. She was right. This one and Trixie were almost *identical*, which meant that whoever had made them had made *two*. Why?

She'd never questioned before where her doll had come from. Trixie was in what few photographs she'd seen of her childhood, her doll locked under her arm almost like an extension of herself.

Like hers, this one looked more than thirty years old. The clothing was a little faded, the face even blanker than it had been all those years ago, but not worn and faded like Trixie had been when DJ had lost her.

DJ felt a chill. So who had left this for her?

Someone who'd had this doll—a doll that was identical to hers before Trixie's accident. Someone who'd known there had been two identical dolls. Someone who knew this doll would be meaningful to her.

But why break in to leave it for her tucked under the covers? And why give it to her now? A life on the run had taught her one thing. The people who had left this wanted something from her. They could have mailed it with a note. Unless they had some reason to fear it could be traced back to them?

Regrettably, there was only one person she could ask, someone she hadn't spoken to in seven years. Her father.

She took a couple of deep breaths as she walked back into the living room. She'd left the door open in case she had needed to get out fast, but now she moved to close and lock it.

With her back against the door, she stared at the apartment she'd come to love. She'd made a life for herself here, and just the thought of being forced to give it up—

She was considering what her intruder might want from her when she felt a prick and dropped the doll. Sucking on her bleeding finger, she stared down at the rag doll. The dress had gaped open in the back to expose a straight pin—and what looked like the corner of a photograph.

Carefully picking up the doll so it didn't stick her again, she unpinned the photo and pulled it out. There were three people in the snapshot. A man and two women, one young, one older, all dark-haired. The young woman, the only one smiling, was holding a baby.

She flipped the photo over. Written in a hurried hand were the words: *Your family.*

What? She quickly turned the photograph back over and stared at the people pictured there.

She'd never seen any of them before, but there was something familiar about the smiling woman holding the baby. DJ realized with a start that the woman looked like her. But how was this possible if her mother had died in childbirth?

If it was true and these people were family…was it possible she was the baby in the photo? Why would her father have lied if that were the case? He knew how much she would have loved having family. He'd always said it was just the two of them. But what if that wasn't true?

Still, she thought as she studied the photo, if it was true, wouldn't they have contacted her? Then she realized they *were* contacting her now. But why wait all these years, and why do it like this?

The reason hit her hard. No one had wanted her to know the truth.

But someone had decided to tell her.

Or *warn* her, she thought with a shiver.

Chapter Two

"Are you sure it's the same doll? I thought you lost it years ago."

DJ gripped the utilitarian standard black phone tighter as she looked through the thick Plexiglas in the prison visiting room at her father.

Walter Justice had been a big, handsome man who'd charmed his way out of trouble all his life—until it caught up with him one night when he'd gotten involved in a robbery that went badly and he ended up doing time for second-degree murder. He had aged well even in prison, and that charm was still there in the twinkle of his blue eyes, in his crooked-toothed smile, in the soft reassuring sound of his voice.

She hadn't been able to wait until visiting day, so this was the best that could be done on short notice with the prison warden. But as surprised and pleased as her father had been to see her, he'd given the doll only a cursory look.

"It's the same doll," she said impatiently into the phone. "It's just not *mine*. Apparently someone made two of these dolls. The clothes are handmade—just like my doll. Everything is identical except the doll isn't mine," she explained impatiently. "So whose is it?"

"How should *I* know?"

"You have to know where *my* doll came from," she argued.

"DJ, you don't really expect me to remember where we picked up a rag doll all those years ago, do you?"

"Yes, I do." She frowned, remembering a photo she'd seen of when she was a baby. Trixie had been lying next to her. "I had it from as far back as I can remember. You should remember if someone gave it to me when I was a baby."

He glanced away for a moment. "Look, if you think it is some kind of threat, then maybe you should disappear for a while."

She hadn't said she thought it was a threat. Her eyes widened in both alarm and anger. What wasn't he telling her?

"That is all you have to say? *Run?* Your answer to everything." She thought of the cheap motels, the carryout food, the constantly looking over her shoulder, afraid someone would either kill her father or take him from her. First sign of trouble—and there was always trouble when your father is a con man—

and off they would go, usually in the middle of the night. She'd spent too many years on the run with him as a child. This time she wasn't running.

"No," she said, gripping the phone until her fingers ached. "This time I want answers. If you don't tell me, I'll get them on my own."

"I only want you to be…safe."

"*Safe?* So this doll *is* a threat." She cursed under her breath. For years she'd had to deal with people her father had swindled or old partners he'd short-changed or screwed over. Half the time she didn't know who was after them or why they had to keep moving, always on the run from something. She'd felt as if she'd had a target on her back all her life because of this man. "What have you gotten me into now?"

"You can't believe this doll is my doing."

Why had she thought that her father, a man who lied for living, would be honest with her? Coming here had been a mistake, but then again, she'd had no one else to ask about the doll—or the photo.

She reached into her pocket. She'd come too far to turn around and leave without at least trying to get the truth out of him. "Who are these people in this photograph, and why would someone want me to have it?" she demanded as she pressed the crinkled photo against the Plexiglas between them.

DJ watched all the color drain from his face. Growing up, she'd learned to tell when he was lying. But what she saw now on his face was pain and fear.

His gaze darting away from the photo as he lowered his voice. "I don't know what this is about, but what would it hurt if you just got out of town for a while?"

She shook her head. "Stop lying to me. You recognize these people. Tell me the truth. Is this my mother? Don't you think I noticed that she looks like me? Am I that baby?"

"DJ, how is that possible? I told you, your mother died in childbirth."

"Then this woman isn't my mother?"

"On my life, you aren't the baby in that photo." He crisscrossed his heart. "And those people are not your family."

She'd been so hopeful. She felt like crying as she peeled the photo off the grimy glass and dropped it back into her bag along with the doll. She'd had to leave her gun in her car and felt naked without it. "But you did recognize the people in the photo."

He said nothing, which came as little surprise.

"I have no idea why I came here." She met his gaze. "I knew you'd lie."

"DJ, whatever you think of me, listen to me now," he pleaded.

DJ. That had been his nickname for her, and it had stuck. But hearing him say it had her fighting tears. She'd once thought her father was the most amazing man in the world. That had been a very long time ago.

She got to her feet, shaking her head at her own naïveté as she started to put the phone back. She'd fallen for his promises too many times in her life. She'd made a clean break when he'd gone to prison, telling him she never wanted to see him again.

Drawing the phone to her ear, she said, "It is clear to me that you've lied to me my whole life. What I don't know is why. But I'm going to find out."

"I did the best I could, just the two of us," her father said, his voice breaking. "I know I could have done better, but, DJ—"

She'd heard this before and couldn't bear to hear it again. "If I have family—" Growing up, she'd often dreamed of a big, boisterous family. Now, with Christmas coming, she felt nostalgic. If she had family, if that's why they'd left this for her now…

She'd seen an ad in a magazine of a family around a beautifully decorated tree on Christmas morning. That night she'd prayed to the starlit night that she could be that little girl in the ad.

But her prayer hadn't been answered, and now she no longer believed in fairy tales. If anything, life had taught her that there were no happy endings.

"DJ, you have to listen to me." He'd raised his voice. The guard was making his way down the line of booths toward him. "You don't know how dangerous—"

"Dangerous?" she echoed.

The guard tapped him on the shoulder. "Time to go."

"DJ—"

"Just tell me the truth." She hated how vulnerable she sounded. She'd seen his face when he'd looked at the people in the photograph. He *had* recognized them. But if they were her family, then why had he looked so…hurt, and yet so frightened? Because he'd been caught in a lie? Or because she had something to fear from them?

She'd had to become strong and trust her own instincts for so long… Growing up on the run with her father had taught her how to survive.

That was, until she'd found the doll and the photo of three people she didn't know, one of them holding a baby who, no matter what he said, was probably her. But what about that would put her in danger?

"Last chance," she said into the phone.

The guard barked another *"Time to go."*

Her father's gaze locked with hers. She saw pleading in his eyes as he quickly said into the phone, "There's a reason I lied all these years, but the truth is…you will be hearing from my family in Montana soon. Go to them until you hear from me." The guard grabbed the phone from her father's hand and slammed it down.

DJ stood staring at him, his words rooting her to the floor. Her father had family in Montana? *She* had family? A family that would be contacting her? If this was another lie…

Slowly she hung up her phone as she watched Walter Justice being led away. Frowning, she pulled out the photo. He's sworn these people weren't her family. Then who were they? Her mother's family? A cold dread filled her at the memory of her father's reaction to the photo.

The doll and the photo proved that they knew about her. That at least someone in that family wanted her to know about them. And now she was going to find them. That she was on her own was nothing new.

And yet the fear she'd seen in her father's eyes almost burned through her resolve.

In Big Sky, Montana, Dana Cardwell Savage braced herself as she pushed open the door to her best friend Hilde's sewing shop. Christmas music played softly among the rows and rows of rich bolts of fabric. For a moment she slowed to admire the Christmas decorations that Hilde had sewn for the occasion, wishing she had time to sew. She missed quilting and the time she used to spend with Hilde back when they were partners in Needles and Pins.

Seeing her friend at the back, she moved on reluctantly. She needed to tell Hilde the news in person. Her only fear was how her friend was going to respond. Their relationship had taken a beating three years ago. Hilde had only begun to trust her again. And now this.

"Dana!" Hilde saw her and smiled, clearly pleased to see her. Raising four children, Dana rarely got down to the shop that she and Hilde had started together. Hilde had bought her out long since then, but Dana still loved coming down here, where it was so peaceful and quiet.

She moved to the stools by the cash register and pulled one up to sit down. There were several people in the shop, but fortunately, Hilde's assistant, Veronica "Ronnie" Tate, was helping them.

"Where are the kids?" Hilde asked.

"With Stacy." She loved that her older sister was so good about taking all of the children to give Dana a break. Stacy's daughter, Ella, was almost five now. Dana's twins were four, Mary was eight and her oldest, Hank, was nine. Where had those years gone?

"So, you're out on the town?" Hilde asked and then seemed to notice how nervous Dana was. "What is it? What's happened?"

"My cousin Dee Anna Justice, the *real* one. Except apparently she goes by DJ. I talked to my uncle, Walter, whom I was led to believe was dead." She didn't want to bias Hilde against the real Dee Anna Justice any more than she might already be, given the past. But she also couldn't keep anything from her. "Walter called from prison."

"Prison?"

Dana nodded. "He assured me that his daughter is nothing like him. In fact, she hadn't talked to him in years until recently. She doesn't know she has family, he said. She was never told about us. My uncle was hoping that I would contact her and invite her to come to Montana for the holidays so she can get to know her family."

Paling, Hilde's hand went to her protruding stomach and the baby inside her. Three years ago, a young woman claiming to be Dee Anna had come to the ranch. Dana, who had so desperately wanted to connect with a part of her family she hadn't known even existed, had fallen for the psychopathic, manipulative woman's lies, and they had all almost paid with their lives.

But Hilde had suffered the most. Dana still couldn't believe that she'd trusted the woman she thought was her cousin over her best friend. She would never forgive herself. The fake Dee Anna, it turned out, had been the roommate of the real Dee Anna Justice for a short period of time. The roommate had opened a piece of her mail and, since they resembled each other, had pretended to be Dee Anna. Dana had believed that the woman was the real Dee Anna Justice and almost lost everything because of it.

"Why would he keep something like that from her?" Hilde finally asked.

"Because his family had disowned him when he

married a woman they didn't approve of. He thought his family would turn both him and his daughter away, apparently."

"But now?"

"Now, he said with Christmas coming, he hoped I would reach out to her and not turn her away as his family had done. She doesn't have any other family, he said." She saw Hilde weaken.

"I told my uncle about the woman who pretended to be Dee Anna. He was so sorry about what happened," Dana said quickly. "He said he'd never met DJ's former roommate, but that he was shocked, and his daughter would be, too, to learn that the woman was capable of the horrible things she did."

Hilde nodded. "So, you've contacted her?"

"No, I wouldn't do that without talking to you first."

Her friend took a breath and let it out. "It's all right."

"I won't if it upsets you too much," Dana said, reaching for Hilde's hand.

"You're sure this time she's the real Dee Anna Justice?"

"Hud ran both her and her father through the system. She has been working as a travel writer, going all over the world to exotic places and writing about them under the pen name DJ Price." One of the perks of being married to the local marshal was that he wouldn't let anyone else come to visit without first finding out his or her true identity.

"So Colt knows that the real Dee Anna has turned up?"

The only good thing that had come out of that horrible time three years ago was Deputy Marshal Colt Lawson. He had believed what Hilde was saying about the fake Dee and had ended up saving her life as well as Dana's and the kids'. Now the two were married, and Dana had never seen Hilde looking happier, especially since she was pregnant with their first child.

"I talked to Colt *first*. He said it was up to you, but none of us wants to take any chances with this baby or your health."

Hilde smiled. "I'm as healthy as a horse and the baby is fine. As long as we're sure this woman is the real Dee Anna and not a murdering psychopath."

The other Dee, the fake Dee Anna Justice, had set her sights on Dana's husband, Marshal Hud Savage, planning to replace Dana. So Dana and her children had to go, and Hilde, the interfering friend in the woman's mentally disturbed mind, along with them. Dana shivered at the memory.

She had nightmares sometimes, thinking they were all still locked in that burning barn. "*That* Dee Anna is dead and gone."

Hilde nodded. "But not forgotten."

"No, not forgotten. It was a lesson I will never forget, and neither will Hud." She smiled and squeezed her friend's hand. "I'm just glad you and I are okay."

"We're more than okay. I know how much family means to you. Contact your cousin and tell her she's welcome. I would never stand in the way of you finding more of your relatives on your mother's side."

"I want you to meet her. If for any reason you suspect anything strange about her—"

Hilde laughed. "I'll let you know if she tries to kill me."

Chapter Three

Beau Tanner had always known the debt would come due, and probably at the worst possible time. He'd dreaded this day since he was ten. Over the years he'd waited, knowing there was no way he could deny whatever request was put to him.

The sins of the father, he thought as he stared at the envelope he'd found in his mailbox this morning. The return address was for an attorney in San Diego, California. But the letter inside was from a California state correction facility prisoner by the name of Walter Justice.

He wondered only idly how the man had found him after all these years, forgetting for a moment the kind of people he was dealing with. Beau could have ended up anywhere in the world. Instead, he'd settled in the Gallatin Canyon, where they'd first met. He suspected Walter had kept track of him, knowing that one day he would demand payment for the debt.

The letter had been sent to his home address here

on the ranch—instead of his office. So he knew before he opened it that it would be personal.

Telling himself just to get it over with, Beau studied the contents of the envelope. There were two sheets of paper inside. One appeared to be a travel article about Eleuthera, an island in the Bahamas. The other was a plain sheet of paper with a printed note:

Take care of my daughter, DJ. Flight 1129 from LA arriving in Bozeman, Montana, Thursday at 2:45 p.m. Dana Cardwell Savage will be picking her up and taking her to Cardwell Ranch. I highly advise you not to let her know that you're watching out for her—and most especially that it was at my request.

It was signed W. Justice.

Under that he'd written, "Cell phone number for emergencies only."

Today was Thursday. DJ's flight would be coming in *this* afternoon. Walter had called it awfully close. What if Beau had been out of town? If he'd questioned whether Walter had kept track of him, he didn't anymore.

He read the letter again and swore. He had no idea what this was about. Apparently Walter's daughter needed protection? A small clue would have been helpful. And protection from what? Or was it from whom?

Also, he was surprised Walt's daughter would be

coming to Montana. That was where their paths had crossed all those years ago. He thought of the dark-haired five-year-old girl with the huge brown expressive eyes and the skinny ten-year-old kid he'd been.

He remembered the way she'd looked up at him, how he'd melted into those eyes, how he'd foolishly wanted to rescue her. What a joke. He hadn't even been able to rescue himself. Like him, she'd been trapped in a life that wasn't her doing.

"Any mail for me?" asked a sleepy-sounding female voice from behind him.

He folded the letter and article and shoved them into his jean jacket pocket before turning to look at the slim, beautiful blonde leaning against his kitchen counter. "Nope. Look, Leah—"

"I really appreciate you letting me stay here, Beau," she said, cutting him off. "If this package I have coming wasn't so important and I wasn't between places right now…"

Beau nodded, mentally kicking himself for getting involved when she'd shown up on his doorstep. "Leah, I wish you hadn't put me in the middle of whatever this is."

"Please, no lectures," she said, raising a hand. "Especially before I've had my coffee. You did make coffee, didn't you? I remember that you always made better coffee than Charlie." Her voice broke at Charlie's name. She turned away from him, but not before he'd seen the tears.

She pulled down a clean cup and poured herself a cup of coffee before turning to him again. He studied her in the steam that rose from the dark liquid. He'd met Leah Barnhart at college when his best friend and roommate, Charlie Mack, had been dating her. The three of them had become good friends. Leah and Charlie had later married and both taken jobs abroad. Over the years, they'd kept in touch for a while, then just an occasional Christmas card. The past few years there hadn't even been a Christmas card.

No wonder he'd been so surprised and caught off guard to find her standing on his doorstep last night.

"And you're not in the middle of anything," she said after taking a long drink of her coffee.

"Why *are* you here?"

"I told you. I'm expecting an important package. I happened to be in Montana and thought about our college days..." She met his gaze and shrugged.

He didn't believe any of it. "Where's Charlie? You said he's still in Europe. I need his number."

She looked away with a sigh. "I don't have it."

He glanced at her bare left-hand ring finger. "Are you *divorced*?"

"No, of course not." She let out a nervous laugh. "We're just— It's a long story, and really not one I'm ready to get into this early in the morning. Can we talk about this later?"

He agreed, since he needed to get to work. DJ Justice would be flying into Montana in a few hours. He had to be ready. He had no idea what was required to keep her safe. It might come down to some extreme measures. Since he didn't know why she even needed protection—or from whom—now was definitely not the time to have a houseguest, especially one who knew nothing about his life before college. He wanted to keep it that way.

"You don't decorate for Christmas?" Leah asked as she looked around the large log home he'd built back in a small valley in the mountains not far from Big Sky. He'd bought enough land that he could have horses—and privacy. That was another reason he'd been surprised to find her on his doorstep. His place wasn't that easy to find.

He raked a hand through his thick, unruly mop of blond hair. "I've never been one for holidays."

She nodded. "I thought you'd at least have had a tree and some lights."

He glanced at his watch. "If you need anything, call my office and talk to Marge."

Leah made a face. "I called your office on my way here. Marge scares me."

He doubted that. He'd known Leah a lifetime ago. Was this woman standing in his kitchen the same Leah he'd toasted when she and Charlie had married? "Marge is a little protective."

"I should say. So you really are a private investigator?"

"That's what my license says."

She studied him with narrowed eyes. "Why do I get the feeling there is more to it?"

"I have no idea," he said. "Are you sure you'll be all right here by yourself?"

"I'll be fine." She smiled. "I won't steal your silverware, if that's what you're worried about."

"I wasn't. Anyway, it's cheap flatware."

She sobered. "I've missed you, Beau. Charlie and I both have. But I honestly do have a package coming here, and it's important or I wouldn't have done it without checking with you first."

"Then we'll talk later," he said and left. It made him nervous, not knowing what was going to be required of him over the next few days or possibly longer—and having Leah here was a complication.

Turning his thoughts again to DJ Justice, he realized he was excited to see the grown-up DJ. He'd thought about her over the years and had hoped her life had turned out all right. But if she was in trouble and needed his help, then there was no way of knowing what her life had been like the past thirty years. He hated to think what kind of trouble she had gotten into that required his help.

Since her father was calling in a promise… Beau was betting it was the dangerous kind.

ANDREI LOOKED AT the coin in his hand for a long moment. His hand shook a little as he tossed the coin and watched it spin before he snatched it from the air and slapped it down on his thick wrist.

He hesitated, mentally arguing with himself. He had a bad feeling this time. But the money was good, and he'd always gone by the flip of a coin.

Superstition dictated that he went through the same steps each time. Otherwise...

He knew too well the *otherwise* as he slowly lifted his palm to expose the coin. Heads, he went ahead with this hit. Tails...

Heads. A strange sense of both worry and disappointment filled him. But the coin toss was sacred to him, so he assured himself he should proceed as he pocketed the coin.

Stepping to the table, he picked up the information he'd been given on the woman he was to kill.

He noticed that a prison snitch had provided her whereabouts. He snorted, shaking his head and trying to ignore that little voice in his head that was telling him this one was a mistake. But he'd worked with the man who'd hired him before, so he pushed aside his doubts and picked up the photo of Dee Anna Justice, or DJ as she was apparently called.

Pretty. He wondered idly what she had done to warrant her death—but didn't let himself stay on that thought long. It had never mattered. It especially couldn't matter this time—his last time.

Maybe that was what had him on edge. He'd decided that this one would be it. With the money added to what he'd saved from the other hits, he could retire at forty-five. That had always been his goal. Another reason he'd taken this job. It would be over quickly. By his birthday he would be home free. He saw that as a sign, since this would be his last job.

Encouraged, he took the data over to the fireplace and lit it with a match. He would already be in Montana, waiting for a sign, by the time Dee Anna Justice arrived.

DJ LEANED BACK into the first-class seat, wishing she could sleep on the airplane. Her mind had been reeling since finding the doll and the photograph. But now, to discover after all these years that she had family, a cousin…

She'd been shocked and wary when she'd gotten the message on her voice mail. *"Hi, my name's Dana Cardwell Savage. I'm your cousin. I live in Montana, where your father was born. I'd really love to talk to you. In fact, I want to invite you to the Cardwell Ranch here at Big Sky for the holidays."*

Instantly she'd known this call had been her father's doing. But how had he gotten her cell phone number? She mentally smacked herself on the forehead as she recalled the guard at the prison searching her purse. The only thing he'd taken was her cell phone, saying she could pick it up on the way out. She should have known her father had friends in prison.

She'd thought about ignoring the message. What if this was just some made-up relative? She wouldn't have put it past her father.

But the voice had sounded…sincere. If this Dana Cardwell Savage really was her cousin…would she be able to fill in the gaps about her father's family? What about her mother's family? Wasn't there a chance she might know something about the doll and photograph?

She'd always had the feeling there was some secret her father had been keeping from her. If Dana Savage had the answer…

After doing some checking, first to verify that Walter William Justice had been born in Montana near Big Sky and then to see if there really was a Cardwell Ranch and a Dana Cardwell Savage, DJ had finally called her back.

A few minutes on the phone and she'd agreed to fly out. "I can't stay for the holidays, but thank you for asking. I would like to meet you, though. I have to ask. What makes you so sure we're cousins?"

Dana explained about discovering an uncle she hadn't known existed until she'd found some old letters from him to her grandparents on her mother's side. "There'd been a falling-out. I hate to say this, but they'd disowned him. That's why I'd never heard of your father until a few years ago, when I found the letters."

His family had disowned him? Was it that simple,

why she'd never known about them? "Do you still have those letters?"

"I do."

She had felt her heart soar. Something of substance she could use to find out the truth. She wanted answers so badly. "I've never known anything about my father's family—or my mother's, for that matter, so I'd love to learn more."

"Family is so important. I'm delighted that your father called. I'd heard he had died. I'm so glad that wasn't true."

Little involving her father was the truth, DJ thought. But if his family had disowned him, then maybe that explained why he'd kept them from her. She had a cousin. How many more relatives did she have that he hadn't told her about?

She tried to relax. Her cousin was picking her up at the airport and taking her to the family ranch where her father had been born. These people were his family, *her family*, people she'd never known had existed until recently. She wanted to pinch herself.

Pulling her purse from under the seat in front of her, she peered in at the rag doll. If only it could talk. Still, looking into its sweet face made her smile in spite of herself. It wasn't hers, but it was so much like hers…

She thought of Trixie and remembered leaving a motel room in the middle of the night and not realizing until later that the doll wasn't with her.

"You must have dropped her," her father had said as they sped out of town.

"We have to go back," she'd cried. "We can't leave her."

He'd looked over at her. "We can't, sweetie. If I go back there... We can't. I'll get you another doll."

She hadn't wanted another doll and had cried herself to sleep night after night until she had no more tears.

"It was just a stupid doll," her father had finally snapped.

"It was all I ever had that was mine."

Now, as she looked at the doll resting in her shoulder bag, she wondered where it had been. Had another girl had this doll as she suspected? But how would that girl know about DJ and Trixie? Trixie was lost, while this doll had been well cared for all these years. Why part with it now?

Her head ached with all the questions and a nagging sense of dread that she wasn't going to like what she found out.

It made no sense that people had given her this doll and the photograph unless they wanted her to find out the truth. But the way they'd left it, breaking into her apartment...

She had tucked the photo into a side pocket of her purse and now withdrew it to study the two women, the one man and the baby in the shot. The man and women were looking at the camera, standing next to a stroller. There was nothing in the background other than an unfamiliar stone wall to give her any idea of where it had been shot—or when.

With a start, she saw something in the photo that she hadn't noticed before. She'd always looked at the people in the photo, especially the woman holding the baby.

But now she saw something in the stroller that made her heart pound. A doll. The doll she now had tucked in her purse. Her father hadn't lied. She *wasn't* this baby, because it wasn't her doll in the stroller. But who was the baby, if not her?

Chapter Four

It had snowed last night, dumping another six inches. Fortunately Highway 191 through the Gallatin Canyon had already been plowed by the time Beau dug himself out and drove to his office on the second floor of an old brick building in downtown Bozeman.

"Good morning, boss," Marge said from behind her desk as he came in. Pushing sixty, solid as a brick wall and just as stout, Marge Cooke was as much a part of Tanner Investigations as the furniture.

"I'm on my way to the airport soon," he said, taking the mail and messages she handed him. "I'll probably be out of contact for a few days," he said over his shoulder as he headed for his office. He heard her get up and follow him.

As he sat down behind his desk, he looked up to find her framed in the doorway. She lifted one dark penciled-in eyebrow and asked, "Since you never take any time off and I know you aren't busy decorating for Christmas, I'll assume you're working. You want me to start a client file?"

"No, this is…personal."

Just when he thought her eyebrow couldn't shoot any higher, it arched toward the ceiling.

"It's not personal like *that*," he said, giving her a shake of his head.

"I have no idea what you're talking about."

He laughed. "I'll be checking in, but I know you can handle things until I get back."

"Whatever you say, boss. Far be it from me to suggest that you haven't been on a date since a Bush was in office."

"Clearly you forgot about that brunette a few months ago."

"That wasn't a date," she said as she turned to leave. "And she made such an impression that you don't even remember her name."

He sat for a moment, trying to remember the brunette's name. Sandy? Susie? Sherry? Not that it mattered, he told himself as he sorted through his mail and messages. He wouldn't be seeing her again.

There wasn't anything in the mail or messages that couldn't keep.

Taking out the letter and the article Walter Justice had sent him, he read them again, then flattened out the article, wondering why it had been included until he saw the travel writer's byline: DJ Price.

So was he to assume that DJ Justice's pseudonym

was Price? He typed DJ Price into his computer's search engine. More articles came up, but no photo of the author. From the dates on the articles it would appear she was still employed as a freelance writer for a variety of publications. If DJ Price was DJ Justice.

He returned the article and letter to the envelope, folded them into his pocket and shut off his computer. As he walked out of his office past Marge's desk, she said, "Shelly," without looking up as he passed. "Wouldn't want you straining your brain trying to remember the woman's name all the way to the airport."

Beau chuckled to himself as he made the drive out into the valley. He couldn't help feeling anxious, since he had no idea what he was getting himself into. Nor did he know what to expect when it came to DJ Justice.

At the airport, he waited on the ground floor by the baggage claim area. There were a half-dozen people standing around holding signs. Dana Savage was one of them. The sign she held up read, CARDWELL RANCH. DJ.

He hung back as the arrivals began coming down from upstairs. On the drive here, he'd told himself there was no way he would be able to recognize DJ. She'd just been a kid of five all those years ago. He'd been a skinny but worn ten.

But the moment he laid eyes on the dark-haired woman at the top of the escalator, he recognized her. Dee Anna Justice. That brown-eyed girl had grown into a striking woman. Her hair was long, pulled back in a loose bun at the nape of her neck. Burnished strands had come loose and hung around her temples.

Silver flashed at her ears and her wrists and throat. She was wearing jeans, winter leather boots that came up to her knees and a teal blue sweater. She had a leather coat draped over one arm, and there was a carry-on in her hand.

She looked up in his direction as if sensing him staring at her. He quickly looked away. This was not what he expected. DJ didn't look like a woman on the run. She looked like a woman completely in control of the world around her.

So what was he doing here?

DJ HAD STILL been upset as the flight attendant announced they would be landing soon. She'd stuffed her purse back under the seat. Out the window, she'd seen nothing but white. Snow blanketed everything. She'd realized with a start that she'd never felt snow. Or had she?

Now she surveyed the small crowd of people waiting on the level below as she rode the escalator down. She knew she was being watched, could feel an intense stare. But when she looked in the direction it came from, she was surprised to see a cowboy.

He stood leaning against the stone wall next to

the baggage claim area. He was dressed in jeans, boots and a red-and-black-plaid wool jacket. His dark Stetson was pulled low, his blond hair curling at the neck of his jacket.

As he tilted his head back, she saw the pale blue familiar eyes and felt a shock before he quickly looked away. There had been a moment of...*recognition*. Or had she just imagined that she knew him? She tried to get a better look at him. Why had she thought she recognized him?

She had no idea.

He was no longer paying any attention to her. She studied his profile. It was strong, very masculine. He held himself in a way that told her he was his own man. He was no urban cowboy. He was the real thing.

She scoffed at the idea that she knew him. She would have remembered a man like that. Still, she couldn't take her eyes off him and was startled when she reached the end of the escalator.

Turning toward the exit, she spotted a woman about her own age holding a sign that said CARDWELL RANCH on it, and in smaller letters, DJ.

The moment her cousin saw her, she beamed with a huge smile. DJ was surprised how that smile affected her. Tears burned her eyes as she was suddenly filled with emotion. She had the crazy feeling that she'd finally come home. Which was ridiculous, since she'd never had a real home life and, as far as she knew, had never been to Montana.

She swallowed the sudden lump in her throat as she wound her way through the small crowd to the young woman. "Dana?"

"DJ?"

At her nod, Dana gave her a quick hug. "Welcome to Montana." She stepped back to stare at DJ. "You don't look anything like the last Dee Anna Justice."

DJ heard relief in her cousin's voice.

"I'm sorry. I shouldn't have said that," Dana said, then must have noticed that DJ didn't know what she was talking about. "Your father did tell you about your former roommate pretending to be you."

"No, I guess he failed to mention that."

"Well, it's water under the bridge… I'm just glad you're here and I finally get to meet you."

"Me, too," DJ said, feeling that well of emotion again.

"We'll get your luggage—"

"This is all I have." Traveling light wasn't the only habit she'd picked up from her father. She had stopped by the bank before she'd left San Diego. She took cash from her safe-deposit box, just in case she might have reason not to use her credit card. But that would mean that she was on the run and needed to hide.

Dana glanced at the overnight bag. "That's it? Not to worry. We have anything you might need. Ready to see the ranch?"

She was. "I'm looking forward to it." Again she

felt someone watching her and quickly scanned the area. It was an old habit from the years when her father used her as a decoy or a lookout.

"Always watch for anyone who seems a little too interested in you—or the ones who are trying hard not to pay you any mind," he used to say.

She spotted the cowboy. He had moved from his spot against the wall and now stood as if waiting for his baggage to arrive. Except he hadn't been on the flight.

"Do you need anything else before we head out?" Dana asked, drawing her attention again.

"No, I'm good," DJ said and followed Dana toward the exit. She didn't have to look back to know that the cowboy was watching her. But he wasn't the only one.

BEAU WATCHED DJ LEAVE, curious if anyone else was watching her. Through the large window, he could see Dana's SUV parked outside. DJ was standing next to it, the two seeming to hit it off.

No one seemed to pay her any attention that he could tell. A few people were by the window, several taking photographs. In the distance, the mountains that surrounded the valley were snowcapped against a robin's-egg-blue sky.

He watched DJ climb into the SUV. As it pulled away, there was the clank of the baggage carousel. The people who'd been standing at the window all turned, pocketing their phones. One man took a moment to send a text before moving to the baggage claim area. Everyone looked suspicious, and no one did.

Beau realized he was flying blind. He had to know why Walter Justice had hired him. He had to know what kind of trouble DJ was in.

Pulling out his phone, he stepped outside into the cold December afternoon. The air smelled of snow. Even with the winter sun shining against the stone wall of the airport, it was still chilly outside.

Beau was glad when the emergency number he'd called was answered. It took a few minutes for Walter to come on the line. He wondered what kind of deal the inmate had made that allowed him such service. Con men always found a way, he thought, remembering his own father.

"Have you seen her?" Walter asked at once.

"I have. But you might recall, I've seen her before."

"She was just a child then."

"She's not now," he said, thinking of the striking woman who'd come down those stairs. "That's just one reason I need to tell her the truth."

"No. That would be a mistake. You don't know her—she doesn't trust anyone."

"Whose fault is that?" Beau asked. "If you want me to get close to her, you have to let me do it my way. Tell me what kind of danger she's in."

"That's just it. I don't know."

Beau swore under his breath. "You expect me to believe that? I have to know what I'm up against." Walter knew enough that he'd "hired" Beau.

Silence filled the line for so long, he feared the inmate had hung up. "It could have something to do with her mother."

"DJ's *mother*?"

"Sorry, not DJ's mother. Carlotta is dead. Her grandmother Marietta is still alive. Marietta might have found DJ."

"Found her?"

"It's complicated."

"I'm sure it is. But if you expect me to keep your daughter safe, you'd better tell me."

There was a sound of clanging doors. Then Walter said, "I have to go. Call me tomorrow." And the man was gone.

Pocketing his phone with a curse, Beau headed for his pickup. He couldn't wait until tomorrow. He would have to do this his way—no matter what Walter Justice had said. He thought of the woman he'd seen. Years ago he'd yearned to save that brown-eyed girl. He was getting a second chance, but he feared he wasn't going to have any more luck than he'd had at ten.

What the hell had he gotten involved in?

DANA CARDWELL SAVAGE was a pleasant surprise. DJ saw at once the family resemblance in this cheerful young woman with the dark hair and eyes. She was so sweet that DJ felt herself relax a little.

"We are so happy to have you here," her cousin was saying. "Your father said that he's been wanting to get us together for years, but with your busy schedule..." Dana glanced over at her and smiled. "I'm glad you finally got the chance. This is the perfect time of year to visit Cardwell Ranch. We had a snow last night. Everything is pretty right now. Do you ski?"

DJ shook her head.

"That's all right. If you want to take a lesson, we can certainly make that happen. But you ride, your father said."

"Ride?"

"Horses. It might be too cold for you, but it's always an option."

The SUV slipped through an opening between the mountains, and DJ was suddenly in a wonderland of white. Massive pine branches bowed under the weight of the fresh white snow. Next to the highway, the river was a ribbon of frozen green.

DJ had never seen anything like it. Or had she? At the back of her mind, she thought she remembered snow. The cold, soft flakes melting in her child-sized hand. That sense of wonder.

Dana was telling her about the Gallatin Canyon and some of its history. "I'm sorry," she said after a few minutes. "I talk too much when I'm excited."

"No," DJ said quickly. "I'm interested."

Dana smiled at her. "You are so different from the last Dee Anna Justice who visited us. Sorry. You said you hadn't heard about it."

"What happened?"

DJ listened and shuddered to think that she'd lived in the same apartment with someone like that. "I'm so sorry. I didn't really know her. We shared an apartment, but since my job is traveling, I was hardly there."

Her cousin waved that off. "Not your fault. That's why we're excited finally to meet the real you."

The real you? DJ almost laughed. She hadn't gone by her real name in years. She wasn't sure she even knew the real her.

Chapter Five

Jimmy Ryan could hardly hold still, he was so excited. He couldn't believe his luck as he saw the man come into the bar.

"You bring the up-front money?" he asked the moment the man took the stool next to him at the bar. The dive was almost completely empty this time of day. Still, he kept his voice down. This was serious business.

When the man had told him he was looking for someone with Jimmy's...talents, he'd never dreamed how perfect he was for the job.

"Montana? Hell, I used to live up there, you know, near Big Sky," Jimmy had bragged. He hadn't been there since he'd flunked out of high school after knocking up his girlfriend and being forced into a shotgun marriage, but that was beside the point.

"I remember you mentioning that. That's why I thought of you. So maybe you know the area?" the man had said.

"Like the back of my hand. I might even know the target."

"Ever heard of the Cardwell Ranch?"

Jimmy had felt a chill as if someone had walked over his grave. This *was* too good to be true. "Are you kidding? I used to…date Stacy Cardwell."

"Well, maybe you won't want this one."

As desperate as he was for money, he would have killed anyone they asked, even Stacy herself, though not before he'd spent some quality time with her for old times' sake.

He'd thought it was fate when the man told him the hit was on a woman named DJ Justice, a cousin of the Cardwells. "Don't know her. Don't care even if I did. Just get me some…traveling money and then let me know how you want it handled."

The man had said he'd get back to him, but it had to be done soon. Jimmy had started making plans with what he would do with all that money.

Now, though, he felt his heart drop as he saw the man's expression. "I'm sorry. The client has decided to go with someone else."

"Someone else?" Jimmy cried loud enough that the bartender sent him a look. "Come on," he said, dropping his voice. "I thought I had it? I'm perfect for the job. Shouldn't it be a case of who gets her first? If it's the money—"

"They went with a pro, all right?"

"Excuse me?" Jimmy demanded, mad at the

thought of losing the money and taking it as an insult. "I grew up in Montana. Do you have any idea how many deer I killed? You ever kill a deer?"

"A deer is a lot different than killing a woman." The man threw down some bills on the bar. "For your time." He slid off his stool and started to step away.

"You think that bothers me?" Jimmy had known some women he would have loved to have put a bullet in. He wouldn't even have flinched.

As the man started through the empty bar toward the back door, Jimmy went after him, trotting along beside him, determined not to let him leave without getting the job.

"I'll do it for less than your...pro."

"I don't think money is the issue," the man said without looking at him. "She just wants it done fast."

She? He was thinking jealousy, revenge, a catfight over some man. "So what did this DJ Justice do? Steal some broad's old man?"

The man stopped at the door. Jimmy could tell that he was regretting giving him the details. "Look, forget this one, and maybe the next time I have something..." The man pushed open the door.

"You want to see a pro? I'll show you a pro. I got this one," he called after him. "I'll find her first and I'll be back for the rest of the money."

STACY CARDWELL WIPED her eyes as the movie ended. She couldn't help blubbering, not at the end of a touching love story. Maybe she was a sucker for a happy ending. Not that she expected one for herself. She'd picked the wrong man too many times.

But she was just happy to have her daughter, Ella, who was almost five years old. Ella had the biggest green eyes she'd ever seen and had stolen her heart even before she was born. Sure, Stacy got lonely sometimes, but she had her sister, Dana, and brothers, Jordan and Clay. Jordan just lived up the road. Clay was still in California but visited a couple times a year.

Years ago they'd had a falling-out over the ranch. Stacy still regretted it. But Dana had forgiven her, and now they were closer than ever.

"Hello?"

She quickly turned off the television as Burt Olsen, the local mailman, stuck his head in the front door of the main ranch house, where Stacy was curled up watching movies.

"Got a package for Dana," he said. "Need a signature."

Stacy waved him on into the house, smiling as he stomped snow off his boots on the porch before entering. Burt was always so polite. Dana was convinced that Burt had a crush on Stacy, but he was just too shy to ask her out. She was glad Dana wasn't herc to tease her about him.

"How's your day going?" Burt asked, then quickly lowered his voice. "The kids asleep?"

She laughed and shook her head. "That would be some trick, to get them all to take naps at their ages. No, their grandpa took them sledding. I'm just holding down the fort until my sister gets back."

"Saw your car out front," Burt said. "Figured you might be sitting the kids. What'd ya think of that snow last night? Really came down. I've already been stuck a couple of times today. Glad I have chains on my rig."

She nodded as she signed for the package. "Can I fill up your thermos with coffee? I have a pot going."

"That would be right nice of you," Burt said, blushing a little. He was a big man with a round red face and brown eyes that disappeared in his face when he laughed. He wasn't handsome by anyone's standards, but there was a warmth and a sincerity about him.

"He will make some woman a fine husband," Dana had said more than once. "A smart woman would snatch him up."

Stacy had never been smart when it came to men, and her sister knew it. But she liked Burt. If she had been looking for a husband... But she wasn't.

When he returned from his truck with the thermos, she took it into the big farmhouse kitchen and proceeded to fill it with hot strong coffee. Burt had followed her only as far as the kitchen doorway.

"Having electrical problems?" Burt asked.

She turned to frown. "No, why?"

"I saw some feller up a pole not far from the house."

Stacy shrugged. "Here, I made sugar cookies. I'll put a couple of them in a bag for you."

"Oh, you don't have to…"

"Dana would insist if she was here," Stacy said.

"Well, thank you." He took the thermos and the plastic bag. "Shaped like Christmas trees," he said, holding up the bag to see the cookies. "You did a real nice job on them."

She felt her cheeks heat. Burt was so appreciative of even the smallest kind gesture a person did for him. "Thank you."

"Well, I'll be getting along, then." He nodded, not quite looking at her. "Might want to dig out some candles in case that lineman turns off your power. You have a nice day now."

"I'm going to try." She watched him drive away, wondering when Burt was going to get around to asking her out and how she was going to let him down easy.

In the kitchen, she got herself some cookies and milk. Going back to the television, she found another Christmas love story and hoped Burt was wrong about the power man cutting off her television. She didn't get that much time alone to watch.

But this show didn't hold her attention. She wondered when Dana would be back with their cousin Dee Anna Justice and what surprises this cousin might bring to the ranch.

As Beau climbed into his SUV and began the drive out of the airport on the newly constructed roads, his cell phone rang. The roads were new because Gallatin Field was now the busiest airport in the state. "Beau Tanner."

"What is your hourly rate?"

He recognized Leah's voice and imagined her standing in his living room. "You can't afford me. Seriously, what is this about?"

"I lied to you. Charlie and I...we're in trouble."

Beau wasn't surprised. "So, there isn't an important package?"

"There is, kind of. I hate involving you in this."

"I can't wait to hear what this is exactly, but can we talk about it when I get home?"

"Yes. But I insist on hiring you. I have money, if that's what you're worried about."

"That isn't it. I have something right now that is going to take all of my attention."

He got off the call, cursing under his breath. If this was about marital problems between her and Charlie...

He really couldn't deal with this right now. Ahead he could see Dana Cardwell's black Suburban heading toward Big Sky. Beau followed, worried about Leah and Charlie, even more worried about DJ Justice.

What kind of trouble was DJ in? Her father thought it might have something to do with her grandmother? That her grandmother had *found* her?

He cursed Walter. Who knew how many skeletons the man had in his closet?

But what did that have to do with his daughter?

If Beau had to lay money down on it, he would have bet there was a man in DJ Justice's story. A man with a jealous wife or girlfriend? Or had DJ chosen a life of crime like her father? At least Beau's father had reformed somewhat after that night here in the canyon when Beau had made the deal with Walter Justice.

Since becoming a private investigator, he'd thought he'd heard every story there was. Where it got dangerous was when the spouse or lover would do anything to cover up an affair—or even a score. Usually money was involved. And passion.

So what was DJ's story?

Marietta Pisani stood at her mirror, considering the almost eighty-year-old woman she saw reflected there. *Merda!* She looked as cranky as she felt, which almost made her smile. When had she gotten so old? She didn't feel all that different than she had in her twenties, except now her long, beautiful, raven-black hair was gray. Her once-smooth porcelain skin was wrinkled.

She knew what had aged her more than the years—her only child, Carlotta. That girl had seemed determined to drive her crazy. It had been one thing after another from an early age. She shook her head, remembering the hell Carlotta had put her through, and then softened her thoughts as she was reminded that her beautiful, foolish daughter was in her grave.

Not that she hadn't left a storm in her wake. And now Marietta had to clean it up.

"Can I get you anything else, Mrs. Pisani?" asked a deep, elderly voice behind her.

She glanced past her reflection in the mirror to Ester, who'd been with her for almost fifty years. Ester had grayed since she'd begun working here as a teen. Sometimes Marietta mixed her up with her mother, Inez, who'd been her first housekeeper right after her marriage.

"No, Ester, I don't need anything."

"What about you, Mr. Douglas?" Ester asked Marietta's solicitor.

Roger shook his head. "I'll be leaving shortly."

"You can turn in," Marietta told the housekeeper.

"Just ring." The sixty-seven-year-old woman turned to leave. "Sleep well." She'd said the same thing every night for the past fifty years.

As Ester closed the door behind her, Marietta focused again on her own reflection. Nothing had changed except now her brows were knit into a deep frown. Ester hadn't been herself lately.

The thought caused Marietta a moment of alarm. Was the woman sick? Marietta was too old to train another housekeeper. Not that Ester kept house anymore. A housecleaning crew came in once a week, and she employed a full-time cook, as well. Ester's only job now was to see to her mistress.

Of course, Ester didn't see it that way. She resented the housekeeping crew and the cook and often sent the cook home early so she could take over the kitchen. She would then make Marietta's favorite meals, just as her mother had done.

The thought that Ester might leave her for any reason was more than she could stand. Ester was the only person in the world Marietta trusted—other than her granddaughter Bianca. She tried to put her worries aside, assuring herself that she'd be dead before Ester went anywhere.

Still, it nagged at her. Not that Ester had said anything. It was more of a...feeling that something was wrong. Unfortunately she knew nothing about the woman's personal life—or if she even had one. Ester had married some worthless man years ago, but she'd had the good sense to get rid of him early on. Since then, as far as Marietta knew, there was no one else in her life. Ester had doted on her and Carlotta and thought that the sun rose and set with Bianca.

When Carlotta had died a few months ago, Ester had taken it harder than Marietta. The housekeeper had loved that child as if she were her own. She'd helped raise her and was the first to make excuses when Carlotta got into trouble, which was often.

But the one Ester loved even more than life itself was Bianca.

It was her thirty-four-year-old granddaughter Marietta worried about now because of Carlotta's deathbed confession.

She clenched her gnarled hands into fists at the memory. The stupid, stupid girl. The secret she'd kept from them all could destroy the legacy Marietta had preserved for so many years—not to mention what it could do to the family fortune.

That was why the mess her daughter had left behind had to be cleaned up. For the family's sake. For Bianca's sake and the generations to come.

"I should go," Roger said.

She'd forgotten he was even still in the room. A slight man with an unmemorable face, he practically disappeared into the wallpaper. "You're sure you can handle this properly?" she asked as she looked past her own image to his.

He sighed. "Yes."

"I don't want Bianca ever to know. If that means paying this woman to keep quiet—"

"I told you I would take care of it. But it is going to cost you. Your daughter left us little choice unless you want to see your family's reputation destroyed by a complete stranger."

A complete stranger. That was what Dee Anna Justice was to her. Marietta had never laid eyes on this...granddaughter, hadn't even known she existed until her daughter's deathbed confession. "Just see that it's done and spare me the sordid details."

"Don't I always?" As he started to leave, she heard a rustling sound and looked up in time to see Ester skittering away.

DANA WAS TELLING her about the "canyon," as the locals called the Gallatin Canyon. It ran from just south of Gallatin Gateway almost to West Yellowstone, some fifty miles of twisting road that cut through the mountains. Sheer rock cliffs overlooked the highway and the Gallatin River.

The drive was breathtaking, especially for DJ, who'd never been in the mountains before—let alone in winter. The winding highway followed the river, a blue-ribbon trout stream, up over the Continental Divide.

"There used to be just a few places in the canyon, mostly ranches or dude ranches, a few summer cabins, but that was before Big Sky," Dana was saying.

DJ could see that luxury houses had sprouted up along the highway as they got closer to the ski resort and community that had grown around it.

"Our ranch was one of the first," her cousin said with obvious pride. "It is home. The only one I've known. And I have no intention of ever leaving it."

DJ couldn't imagine what it must have been like living her whole life in one place.

Dana slowed and turned not far past the sign for Big Sky Resort. Across the river and a half mile back up a wide valley, the Cardwell Ranch house sat against a backdrop of granite cliffs, towering snow-filled pines and bare-limbed aspens. The house was a big, two-story rambling affair with a wide front porch and a brick red metal roof. Behind it stood a huge new barn and some older outbuildings and corrals.

"Hud, my husband, keeps saying we need to build a bigger house, since we have four children now. But…well…"

"It's wonderful," DJ said and tried to imagine herself growing up here.

"You'll be staying in one of our guest cabins," her cousin said and pointed to some log buildings up on the side of the mountain. "I think you'll be comfortable there, and you'll have your privacy."

DJ was overwhelmed by all of it, so much so that she couldn't speak. As Dana parked, a dark-haired woman came out on the porch to greet them.

"Stacy," Dana called. "Come meet our cousin."

Chapter Six

DJ thought Stacy looked like an older version of her sister. She'd been prettier at one time, but her face told of a harder life than Dana had lived. Seeing how much she resembled both of her cousins gave DJ a strange feeling. For once, her father had told the truth. These people were her *family*.

Dana introduced them and then asked her sister, "How were the kids?"

"Dad came by and took them sledding," Stacy said. "He called just before you drove up to say he's decided to take them to Texas Boys Barbecue, since they say they're too starved to wait for supper. The café is owned by our cousins from Texas," she said to DJ. Turning back to her sister, she said, "I'm working this afternoon at the sewing shop, so I'd better get going, since I need to pick up a few things before then."

"Go, and thanks."

Stacy looked to DJ, who'd been taking in the

ranch in a kind of awe. "It was great to meet you. I'll see you later?"

"You'll see her. DJ's staying for a while," Dana declared and climbed the porch steps to open the door and usher DJ in.

She stepped into the house and stopped. The decor was very Western, from the huge rock fireplace to the antler lamps and the Native American rugs on the hardwood floors. Even the Christmas decorations looked as if they'd been in the family for years.

There was also a feeling of déjà vu as if she'd been here before. Crazy, she thought, hurriedly wiping at her eyes.

"It's so…beautiful," DJ said, her voice breaking.

Dana laughed. "*My Christmas tree?* I know it's hard to put into words," she said, considering the misshaped evergreen in the corner, decorated with ornaments obviously made by children. "But I've always been a sucker for trees that would never have gotten to be Christmas trees if it wasn't for me."

DJ managed to laugh around the lump in her throat. "I meant your house," she said, smiling at the sight of the ungainly tree, "but your Christmas tree is…lovely. An orphan tree that you brought home. It's charming."

Her cousin smiled at her. "Let's have a late lunch, since I know you couldn't have gotten much on the plane, and we can visit."

She followed Dana into the large, cheery kitchen,

wondering if she hadn't been here before. It felt strangely…familiar. Had her father brought her here at some point? Why else was she feeling so emotional about this large, rambling old house?

"I can't tell you how surprised I was when I found some letters from your father and realized that my mother had a brother I'd never known existed," Dana said as she opened the refrigerator and pulled out a large bowl. "I hope you like shrimp macaroni salad." DJ nodded and Dana continued. "It wasn't like my mother, Mary Justice, to keep a secret like that. Then to find out that he hadn't actually died…" Her cousin put the bowl on the table and got out plates, forks and what looked like homemade rolls. "Coffee, tea, milk?"

"Milk." She couldn't remember the last time she'd had milk, but it sounded so good, and it felt right in this kitchen. Everywhere she looked she saw family history in this house. One wall was covered with photos of the children, most atop horses.

"Sit, please." Dana waved her into one of the mismatched multicolored wooden chairs in front of the long, scarred table.

"I didn't know about you, either," DJ said as she pulled out the chair and sat. Dana joined her after filling two plates with pasta salad. DJ took a bite. "This is delicious."

They ate in a companionable silence for a while. The house was warm and comfortable. From the window over the sink, DJ could see snow-laden pines and granite cliffs. It was all so beautiful, exactly how she had pictured Montana in December. She hadn't thought she was hungry, but the salad and the warm homemade roll dripping with butter quickly disappeared. This felt so right, being here, that she'd forgotten for a while why she'd accepted the invitation.

DJ was running her finger along one of the scars on the table when Dana said, "I can't understand why my grandparents would disown their son the way they did. They were a lot older when they had your father. Maybe it was that generation…but not to tell us…"

DJ took a sip of cold milk before she asked, "Who told you he was dead?"

"I didn't speak to your mother personally, but her assistant—"

"My *mother's assistant*?" DJ asked, abruptly putting down her milk glass. "When was this?"

Her cousin thought for a moment. "That would have been in the spring three years ago. Her assistant, at least, that's who she said she was, told me that your mother couldn't come to the phone."

"I was always told that my mother's been dead since I was born," DJ said. "It's what I've believed all my life, so I don't understand this."

"I don't understand it, either. Then whose assistant did I speak with, if not Marietta Pisani's?"

"She told you my mother's name was Marietta?"

She shook her head. "Where did you get the number to call her?"

"From…from the woman who'd pretended to be you, Camilla Northland. After she was caught, I asked her where the real Dee Anna Justice was. I thought she was telling me the truth." Dana put a hand over her mouth. "Why did I believe anything that woman told me? I feel like such a fool."

"No, please don't. So my roommate gave you the number?"

Dana nodded. "She said a woman had called the apartment asking for you before she left to come out here to Montana to pretend to be you. When your roommate asked who was calling, she said her name was Marietta."

"That's my grandmother's name, but she is also deceased. At least, that's what my father told me. But since he kept all of you from me…" Her life felt like one big, long lie. "My father told me that my mother's name was Carlotta."

Her cousin looked flummoxed. "Camilla seemed to think Marietta was your mother. Either she lied, or—"

"Or the person who called lied."

Dana nodded thoughtfully. "I believed Camilla, since she also told me that the reason my uncle had been disinherited was that he'd married a foreigner. The woman who said she was Marietta's assistant had an Italian accent. I asked about her daughter.

I'm not even sure I called you by name. She said you were in Italy—or was it Spain?—visiting friends. Is any of this true?"

DJ shook her head. "I've been in San Diego all this time except when I was traveling for work. I have no idea where my former roommate could have gotten her information, but that she knew my grandmother's name... I don't think she was lying about the phone call. Do you still have that number?"

Dana shook her head. "I'm sorry."

"I was hoping you could help me piece together more of my family history. My father told me that he and I were the only two left. Until he told me that you might be calling, I had no idea that wasn't true."

"Well, you have me and Stacy, plus my brothers, Jordan and Clay, as cousins, plus our cousins from Texas. You'll meet Jordan tonight. Clay lives in California, not that far from where you live now. So, you never met anyone on your mother's side of the family?"

"No. All I knew was that my mother's name was Carlotta and my grandmother's was Marietta. My father's never been very...forthcoming with information. He let me believe I didn't have *any* family."

"Oh, DJ, I'm so sorry," Dana said, reaching across the table to take her hand. "Family is...my heart. My father and uncle, my father-in-law, are often... trying," she said and smiled. "I've fought tooth and nail with my siblings, lost them for a few years, but finally have them back. I can't imagine not having any of them in my life. I'm so glad that now you have all of us."

DJ's eyes burned as she squeezed her cousin's hand.

"All of us *and* Cardwell Ranch," Dana added and let go of her hand.

DJ picked at her lunch for a moment. Was it possible that her grandmother Marietta was still alive? Then wasn't it also possible that her mother, Carlotta, was alive, as well? She could see why her father might have kept her from his family, since they had disinherited him, but why had he kept her from her mother's family?

DJ remembered the night she'd finally badgered her father into telling her about her mother. He'd had too much to drink. Otherwise all he'd ever said was that her mother had died and it was too painful to talk about. That night, though, he told her that Carlotta had been a beautiful princess and the love of his life.

"She was too beautiful," he'd said. "Too spoiled, too rich, too much of everything. Her family didn't think I was good enough for her. They were right, of course." He'd let out a bitter laugh. "It cost me my family as well, but I will never regret loving her." He'd blinked back tears as he looked at DJ. "And I got you. I'm a lucky man."

She'd been full of questions. How could he have lost Carlotta and his family, too?

"Do you understand now why I don't want to talk about your mother? So, no more," he'd said with a wave of his hand. "I can't bear it." His gaze softened as it fell on her. "Let's just be grateful that we have each other, because it's just you and me, kid."

Even now, she couldn't be sure any of his story was true. Her heritage was a puzzle with most of the pieces missing. "I'm surprised that you'd never heard of my father before you found the letters," she said.

"I was shocked. Like I said, I still can't believe my mother would have kept something like that a secret."

"You said you still have those letters?"

"I can dig them out, along with that number—" At the sound of a vehicle, followed by the eruption of children's voices, Dana added, "After I corral the kids."

DJ cleaned up the dishes while Dana went to greet the children. She could hear laughter and shrieks of playfulness outside. She couldn't help but smile to herself.

Drying her hands, she pulled out the photo and studied it in the light from the kitchen window. With her cousin's help, she was going to find the family she'd been denied.

She gazed at the photo of the baby—and the doll in the stroller. If she wasn't the baby the smiling woman was holding, then who was, and why had someone wanted her to believe they were family?

Whoever had left her the doll and the photo knew

the truth—and wanted her to know it. But what was the truth? And what was the motive? To help her? Or to warn her?

She felt a sudden chill. She would find out, but at what cost?

ON THE WAY to the small resort town of Big Sky, Stacy couldn't get DJ off her mind. There was a distinct family resemblance because of the dark hair and eyes, but still…she had the feeling that she'd met her when they were kids.

At the drugstore, she got out and was about to lock her car when she heard the sound of footfalls in the new snow behind her.

"Stacy?"

She started at the familiar male voice directly behind her. Turning, she came face-to-face with her old boyfriend from high school. *"Jimmy?"*

He grinned. "I go by James now. I'm surprised you remember me."

How could she not remember Jimmy Ryan? He'd dumped her right before her junior prom to go back to his old girlfriend, Melody Harper. He'd been the first in a long line to break her heart.

"Are you here for the holidays?" He and Melody had gotten married right after high school. Melody, it turned out, had been pregnant. He'd taken a job with Melody's uncle in California, and that was the last Stacy had heard or seen of him.

He was looking at her the way he used to, unnerving her. "I wondered if you were still around."

"I left for a while. How is Melody?"

"Wouldn't know. We're divorced. How about you?"

For a moment she couldn't find her voice. "Divorced." More times than she wanted to admit. "I have a daughter, Ella."

"Lucky you. It turned out that I couldn't have children."

She blurted out in surprise, "But I thought Melody was pregnant."

"Turns out she wasn't," he said bitterly. "She told me that she'd miscarried, so we spent a lot of years trying before the truth came out."

"I'm sorry."

His gaze met and held hers. He was still the most handsome man she'd ever known. His dark hair was salted with gray at the temples, which only seemed to make his gray eyes more intense. "Could I buy you a cup of coffee?"

Stacy felt that old ache. Had she ever gotten over Jimmy? Wasn't he why she'd jumped into one relationship, one marriage after another? "I have to get back to the ranch soon."

"Just a quick cup of coffee. I've thought about you so often over the years and regretted letting you down the way I did."

How many times had she dreamed that he would say those words—or at least words much like them?

She glanced at her watch. "I suppose a cup of coffee wouldn't hurt."

"You're tired from your long trip," Dana said after introducing DJ to all the children and her father, Angus Cardwell. "Dad, if you don't mind staying around for a few minutes, I'm going to take DJ to her cabin so she can get some rest."

"You're in good hands," Angus said. "Trust me."

DJ couldn't help but smile. Trust wasn't something that came easy for her. But Dana and this family inspired trust.

"The kids want to go see a movie in Bozeman," Angus said. "Maybe we'll do that and really make a day of it."

There were cheers from the five children. Dana laughed. "You haven't had enough of them? Fine. But we're all going to The Corral tonight. Stacy has agreed to babysit."

As they stepped outside, DJ on impulse turned to her cousin and hugged her. "Thank you for everything."

"I haven't done anything yet," Dana said. "But I am so glad you're here. Families need to stick together."

With that, her cousin walked her up to her cabin on the mountainside.

DJ couldn't believe the cabin as her cousin opened the door and ushered her in. Someone had started a fire for her. It blazed bright in a fireplace on the other side of a seating area. There was a small kitchen that she knew would be stocked with anything she might need even before Dana opened the refrigerator door to show her.

But it was the bedroom that stole her heart. "Oh, that bed." It was huge, the frame made of logs, the mattress deep in pillows and quilts. "I won't want to get out of it."

Her cousin smiled and pulled out a step. "This is how you get on the bed. I told them it was too high, but my brother Jordan made the beds, and so far everyone loves them."

"I can see why," DJ said, laughing. "This is amazing. Really, thank you so much."

"It's my pleasure. You'll get to meet Jordan and his wife, Liza. Clay, your other cousin, as I told you, lives in California. He'll be flying up for Christmas. But we'll get to all of that." She smiled. "I'm just happy you're here now. We can talk about Christmas later."

"I can only stay for a few days. With the holidays coming, I don't want to be in the way."

"In the way?" Dana exclaimed. "You're family. You'll make this Christmas even more special."

DJ couldn't help being touched.

"Get settled in and rest. We have something special planned for tonight. The Corral has the best burgers you've ever tasted, and the band playing tonight? It's my uncle and father's band—more relatives of yours I thought you'd enjoy meeting in a more casual atmosphere."

Dana was so thoughtful that DJ couldn't say no.

"I'll drop by some clothing and Western boots that should fit you before we go."

DJ started to tell her that this was all too much, but Dana cut her off. "You have to experience Montana and canyon life. I promise that you'll have a good time."

There was nothing more DJ could say, since she didn't want to disappoint her cousin. Dana had been so welcoming, much more than she should have been for a relative she'd never met before.

She watched Dana walk back down to the main house. Something in the distance flashed, the winter sun glinting off metal. She could see a repairman hanging from a power pole in the distance.

Emotional exhaustion pulled at her. The past few days had been such a roller-coaster ride. She closed the door and locked it. For the first time, she felt... safe.

The cabin was so warm and welcoming, she thought as she walked into the bedroom. The bed beckoned to her. Smiling, DJ pulled back the homemade quilt, kicked off her shoes and crawled up under the covers. She was asleep almost at once.

MARIETTA KNEW SHE wouldn't be able to sleep. She kept thinking about this granddaughter. She realized she knew nothing about her other than what Roger had told her. A father in prison. The young woman writing stories for travel magazines.

"Not married?" she'd asked.

"No. Lives alone. Stays to herself."

She tried to imagine the girl. Did she look like Carlotta or that horrible father of hers? What if she looked like Bianca?

Reaching over, she rang the bell for Ester. It was late, but she knew she'd never get to sleep without some warm milk.

"Is something wrong?" Ester asked moments later from her doorway.

"I can't sleep."

"I'm not surprised."

She stared at her housekeeper. "I beg your pardon?"

Ester shook her head. "I'll heat some milk. Would you like anything else?"

Marietta gritted her teeth as she shook her head. It wasn't her imagination. Ester was acting oddly.

When she returned with a glass of warm milk and a biscuit with butter and honey, Marietta asked, "Roger hasn't called, has he?"

"I'm sure you would have heard the phone if he had, but no."

"You don't like him." She realized she'd given voice to something she'd known for a long time. Not that she normally cared if her housekeeper liked her attorney or not. But tonight, it struck her as odd. Almost as odd as the way Ester was behaving.

"No, I don't like him. Nor do I trust him. You shouldn't, either." Ester started to leave.

"Why would you say that?" she demanded of the housekeeper's retreating back.

Ester stopped and turned slowly. "Because he's been stealing from you for years." With that, she left the room.

Marietta stared after her, dumbstruck. Was Ester losing her mind? It was the only thing that made sense. The woman had never talked to her like this. She would never have dared. And to say something so…outrageous.

She took a sip of the milk, followed by a bite of the biscuit, until both were gone. Neither was going to help her sleep tonight.

Chapter Seven

The Corral turned out to be an old-fashioned bar and restaurant that looked as if it had been there for years. DJ liked the idea of a place having a rich history—just like the ranch Dana had grown up on. She couldn't imagine having that kind of roots. Nor could she imagine knowing the same people for years like Dana did—which quickly became obvious as they climbed out of the large SUV.

The parking lot was full of pickups and a few SUVs. Several trucks drove up at the same time they did. The occupants called to Dana and were so friendly that DJ felt a stab of envy.

"Do you know everyone in the canyon?" she asked.

Her cousin laughed. "Hardly. I did once upon a time. But that was before Big Sky Resort."

The moment they walked through The Corral door, the bartender said hello to Dana, who quickly set them both up with light beers. "You're in Montana now," she said, clinking her beer bottle against DJ's. The band broke into an old country song, the lead guitarist nodding to them as he began to sing.

"You already met my father, Angus Cardwell, on lead guitar," Dana said as she led her to the only empty table, one with a reserved sign on it that read Cardwell Ranch. "And my uncle Harlan is on bass tonight. They switch off. They've been playing music together for years. They've had other names, but they call themselves the Canyon Cowboys now, I think." She laughed. "They're hard to keep track of."

They'd barely sat down and had a drink of their beers when Dana's brother Jordan came in with his wife, Liza, a local deputy still in her uniform. Jordan was dark and good-looking and clearly in love with his wife, who was pregnant.

"We came by to say hello, but can't stay long," Jordan said. "I'm sure we'll get to see you again while you're here, though."

"Is your husband coming?" DJ asked after Jordan and Liza had left.

"Hud's working tonight. But you'll get to meet him." Dana ordered loaded burgers as the band kicked into another song. "Oh, there's Hilde." Her cousin rose to greet her very pregnant friend. They spoke for a moment before Dana drew her over to the table.

Hilde looked reluctant to meet her. But DJ couldn't

blame her after everything she'd heard about the pretend Dee Anna Justice.

"I'm so sorry about my former roommate," DJ said. "I had no idea until Dana told me."

Hilde shook her head. "It's just nice that we finally get to meet you. How do you like the ranch?"

"I love it, especially that four-poster log bed I took a nap in earlier."

Hilde laughed as she sat. Her husband came in then, still wearing his marshal's office uniform, and went to the bar to get them drinks.

A shadow fell across the table. When DJ looked up, she was surprised to see the cowboy from the airport standing over her.

"Care to dance?" he asked over the music.

DJ was so startled to see him here that for a moment she couldn't speak.

"Go ahead," Dana said, giving her a friendly push. "Beau Tanner is a great dancer."

Beau Tanner. DJ didn't believe this was a coincidence. "Did you have something to do with this?" she whispered to her cousin.

"Me?" Dana tried to look shocked before she whispered, "Apparently he saw you at the airport and wanted to meet you."

So that was it. DJ pushed back her chair and stood. Maybe his interest in her was innocent. Or not. She was about to find out either way.

He took her hand and pulled her out onto the

dance floor and into his arms for a slow dance. He was strong and sure, moving with ease, and definitely in control.

"Dana told me you would be here tonight," he said. "I was hoping you would dance with me."

"Why is that?" she asked, locking her gaze on his.

His pale blue eyes were the color of worn denim, his lashes dark. Looking into those eyes, she felt a small jolt. Why did she get the feeling that she'd looked into those eyes before?

"I saw you at the airport. When I heard that you were Dana's cousin, I was curious." He shrugged.

"*Really?* You just happened to hear that."

"News travels fast in the canyon."

"What were you doing at the airport? I know you weren't on my flight. I also know you weren't picking anyone up."

He laughed. "Are you always this suspicious?"

"Always."

She lost herself in those eyes.

"You want to know why I was at the airport? Okay." He looked away for a moment before his gaze locked with hers. "Because of you."

"So much for your story that you just happened to see me at the airport and were curious."

"I don't like lying. That's just one reason we need to talk," he said as he pulled her close and whispered into her ear. "Today at the airport wasn't the first time I'd seen you. We've met before."

She drew back to look into his face. "If this is some kind of pickup line…" Even as she said it, she remembered thinking at the airport that he looked familiar. But she was always thinking people looked like someone from her past. That was normal when you had a past like hers.

"It was years ago, so I'm not surprised that you don't remember," he said as the song ended. He clasped her hand, not letting her get away as another song began.

"Years ago?" she asked as he pulled her close.

"You were five," he said next to her ear. "I was ten. It was only a few miles from here in this canyon."

She drew back to look at him. "That isn't possible. I've never been here before." But hadn't she felt as if she had? "Why would I believe you?"

He looked her in the eye. "Because a part of you knows I'm telling the truth. It's the reason you and I need to talk." Without warning, he drew her off the dance floor, toward the front door.

She could have dug her heels in, pulled away, stopped this, but something in his tone made her follow him out the door and into the winter night. He directed her over to the side of the building where snow had been plowed up into a small mountain. "Okay, what is this about?" she demanded, breaking loose from his hold to cross her arms over her chest. "It's freezing out here, so make it fast."

He seemed to be deciding what to tell her. She

noticed that he was watching the darkness as if he expected something out there to concern him. "All those years ago, your father did me a favor," he said.

She laughed, chilled by the night and this man and what he was saying. "Now I know you're lying. My father didn't do favors for anyone, especially for ten-year-olds."

"Not without a cost," he agreed.

She felt her heart bump in her chest and hugged herself tighter to ward off the cold—and what else this man might tell her.

"Your father and mine were…business partners."

"So this is about my father." She started to turn away.

"No, it's about you, DJ, and what your father has asked me to do."

She stared at him. She'd come here wanting answers. Did this man have them? If he was telling the truth, she'd been to Montana with her father years ago. It would explain why some things and some people seemed familiar—including him.

She could see the pale green frozen river across the highway, the mountains a deep purple backdrop behind it. Everything was covered with snow and ice, including the highway in front of the bar.

"If our fathers were business partners, then I don't want anything to do with you."

"I wouldn't blame you, but my father got out of

the…business after the night we met. I'm assuming yours didn't, given that he is now in prison."

She flinched. "How do you know that?"

"I told you. He did me a favor—for a price. He contacted me. It's a long story, but the night we met, your father and I made a deal of sorts. He helped me with the understanding that if he ever needed my help…"

"You said he did a favor for you? My father made a deal with a ten-year-old?"

"I promised to do whatever he wanted if he let my father go."

DJ felt a hard knot form in her chest. "I don't understand." But she feared she did.

"My father had double-crossed yours. Your father was holding a gun to his head."

"And you threw yourself on the sword, so to speak, by promising my father what, exactly?" What could her father have extracted from a boy of ten?

"He asked me to make sure that nothing happens to you."

She laughed, but it fell short. "That's ridiculous. Why would he think *you* could keep me safe?"

"I'm a private investigator. I have an office forty miles away in Bozeman. I'm good at what I do."

"And humble." She rubbed her arms through the flannel shirt her cousin had given her to wear. But it wasn't her body that was chilled as much as her soul. Her father, the manipulator. He'd gotten her here. Now he was forcing this cowboy to protect her?

She shook her head and started to step away again. "I can take care of my—"

A vehicle came roaring into the parking lot. As the headlights swept over them, Beau grabbed her and took her down in the snowbank next to them, landing squarely on top of her.

JIMMY RYAN RUBBED his cold hands together. He'd already spent several hours of his life sitting outside a bar, hoping to get a shot at DJ Justice. Finding out where DJ would be tonight had been child's play. Over coffee with Stacy he'd listened distractedly as she'd told him what she'd been up to since high school.

"So you're living at the ranch?" he'd asked. "How's that working out with family?"

"Fine. Another cousin has turned up. They seem to be coming out of the woodwork," she'd said with a laugh. "First my five male cousins from Texas. They opened Texas Boys Barbecue here in Big Sky. Have you been there yet?"

"Not yet. But you said another cousin has turned up?"

"Dee Anna Justice. DJ. I haven't gotten to spend much time around her and won't tonight. I'm baby-sitting the kids so Dana can take her out."

"Oh, yeah? Your sister taking her to someplace fancy?"

"The Corral. My father and uncle are playing there. You remember that they have a band, right?"

The Corral. "Sure, I remember. So what does this cousin look like?"

She'd described DJ. Sounded like he couldn't miss her, so to speak.

He'd glanced at his watch. "I'm going to have to cut this short. Maybe we can see each other again." If things went right tonight, that wouldn't be happening. But he hadn't minded giving Stacy false hope. And who knew, he'd thought, maybe they could hook up before he left. She was still pretty foxy, and he could tell she still wanted him.

Now, sitting across the highway in his rented SUV, his rifle lying across his lap, he just hoped he got another chance at DJ. Earlier she'd come out of the bar. But she'd been with some man.

He'd still been tempted to take the shot, but the man had stayed in front of her. When a car had come racing into the parking lot, the cowboy had thrown them both in a snowbank. What was that about?

"What in the—" DJ's words were cut off by the sound of laughter as several people tumbled from the vehicle.

"Shh," Beau said, pulling back to look at her. She saw a change in his expression. Still, the kiss took her by more than surprise. She pushed against his hard chest, but his arms were like steel bands around her.

Worse, she felt herself melting into him, into the kiss, into the warmth of his mouth and the taste of beer on his lips. She was vaguely aware of music and laughter and the sound of people as they entered the establishment before he let her go.

She was shaken by the kiss and everything he'd told her as he rose and pulled her to her feet. "What was that?" she demanded as she began to brush cold snow off her backside.

"A kiss. Apparently it's been a while for you, as well," he said with a cockiness that was downright aggravating. He began to help her with the snow, his big hand brushing over the Western shirt, vest and jeans she wore.

"I can do it myself," she snapped and took a step away from him. She wanted to tell him that she'd only kissed him back because he'd taken her by surprise. But he didn't give her a chance to lie.

"Don't look so shocked. It was just a kiss, right?" His blue eyes gleamed in the light from the neon sign over their heads. "It wasn't like you felt anything. Like either of us felt anything."

The man was exasperating. She hadn't come looking for any of this. "I was asking why you thought you could get away with kissing me like that. Or was that part of the bargain you made with my father?" she asked, hoping he caught the sarcasm.

"I wasn't sure who was driving up just then. I was merely doing my job. Protecting you, since the one thing your father didn't make clear is whom I'm protecting you from. As for the kiss, it just seemed like a good idea. It won't happen again."

"You're right about that, because I don't need your so-called protection." With that, she pushed past him and started for the bar as Dana opened the door and called, "DJ, your burger's ready."

JIMMY RYAN WASN'T the only one watching some distance from The Corral. Andrei had learned to be patient, studying his mark, waiting for a sign that the situation was perfect.

He would get only one chance to pull the trigger. Rushing it would put the mark on alert and make his job next to impossible. That's if he didn't get caught trying to get away after blowing it.

He'd seen Dee Anna Justice, or DJ, as she was called, go into the bar with her cousin. He wasn't even tempted to take the shot. Later everyone would have been drinking and that would add to the confusion about where the shot had come from.

He'd been surprised when DJ had come back out so soon—and with a man. They seemed to be in an intense conversation.

Who was this cowboy?

What happened next turned Andrei's blood to ice. A vehicle came roaring into the bar's parking area. The cowboy with Dee Anna threw her into the snowbank next to where they had been talking.

Andrei sat up straighter, tightening his grip on

the binoculars. Why was the cowboy so jumpy? It made no sense.

He swore. Had there been another contract out on her—one that had failed? How else could he explain why the man with her had reacted like that?

What had he gotten himself into?

BEAU STOOD NEXT to the snowbank, cussing under his breath. Walter had warned him not to tell her. Now he understood why. The woman was stubborn as a danged mule.

He touched his tongue to his lower lip and tasted her, smiling as he thought of the kiss. No matter what she'd said, he'd felt her kissing him back.

Another vehicle pulled into the parking lot, dragging him back to the problem at hand. DJ Justice. How was he going to keep her safe? And safe from what? Or whom? He cursed Walter Justice. Tomorrow he would call him back, but in the meantime, all he could do was keep an eye on the man's daughter.

Good luck with that, he told himself as he went back into the bar. She was sitting again with her cousin. He went to the bar, taking a stool where he could watch her in the mirror behind the counter. She looked up and their gazes met for a moment.

She touched her tongue to the corner of her mouth and licked away a dollop of ketchup. Then she smiled as if she knew exactly what that had done to him. It was clear that she understood how their kiss had affected him. Because it had affected her, as well? Not likely.

He pulled his gaze away to nurse his beer. This woman was going to be the death of him.

Chapter Eight

Jimmy cursed and told himself to stay calm. He was going to get his shot. He'd been ready, but the damned man kept blocking his shot. He'd decided to try to take them both out when he got his chance.

He put the crosshairs on her head. His finger teased the trigger. He took a breath. He couldn't blow this.

A semi roared past between him and the bar, kicking up a cloud of snow. When he looked through the scope again, the woman had pulled away from the man and gone back into the bar, the man right behind her. Who was this guy, anyway?

Jimmy swore, hauled his rifle back in and closed his window. He tried not to be discouraged. He had Stacy, which meant he had a standing invitation to Cardwell Ranch. Why rush it? What was another day?

He was getting cold and tired by the time the door of the bar opened again. He put his window down, lifted the rifle and looked through the scope. Two women. He recognized Stacy's sister, Dana, leading the way. Right behind her was…DJ Justice.

His heart began to pound. His finger on the trigger began to shake. Before he could get the crosshairs on her, the door of the Suburban opened and she was gone.

He beat the steering wheel with his fist, then whirred up the window. He'd get his chance. He had to. A thought struck him. He'd find out where DJ was staying on the ranch and take her out quietly, he thought as he tested the blade with his thumb. A bead of blood appeared on his skin at the mere touch.

The idea of cutting her throat appealed to him. He was good with a knife. It would be better this way. Better chance of killing her and then making a clean getaway before anyone was the wiser.

He just had to make sure that the pro didn't get to her first. Maybe their paths would cross. He sheathed the knife, smiling at the prospect of surprising the pro.

DJ WATCHED THE winter landscape sweep past under a full moon. "I really like your friend Hilde."

Dana smiled as she drove them toward the ranch. "I'm so glad. Hilde liked you, too. So, what did you think of Beau Tanner?"

She shot a look at her cousin. "How long have you known him?" she asked, avoiding the question.

"Not all that long. His family is from the canyon, but he returned only about five years ago. You two seemed pretty close when you were dancing."

DJ smiled. "You aren't playing matchmaker, are you? You know I'm going to be in town only a few days."

"You'll be here a lot longer than that if I have my way," Dana said and laughed.

When they reached the house, the porch light was on, but everyone appeared to have gone to bed hours ago.

"I should probably go on up to my cabin," DJ said, getting out of the Suburban.

"I saw that my sister made sugar cookies. I'm thinking cookies and hot cocoa. Interested? It's not that late."

DJ couldn't resist. "If you're sure we won't wake everyone up."

"The kitchen is a long way from the upstairs bedrooms. Come on," she said, leading DJ inside.

A few minutes later, nibbling a sugar cookie, DJ watched her cousin make hot cocoa. Her mind kept returning to Beau Tanner and what he'd told her earlier, not to mention the kiss. That she'd felt something— not just something, but *something*—made her angry with herself. Worse, he'd known she felt it.

But she suspected he had, too. She smiled to herself as she recalled his expression as he'd watched her lick the dab of ketchup from the corner of her mouth.

"DJ?"

She realized she hadn't been listening. "I'm sorry?"

"Do you want me to get out the letters or is it too late?" Dana asked.

"No, I would love it, if you can find them."

"I found them earlier and put them in the desk down here," she said. "I know you're anxious to learn everything you can about your family. Me, too. Pour us each a cup and I'll get them."

DJ filled two mugs with hot cocoa and, with a plate of cookies, sat down at the table. Dana returned, sat down next to her and pushed a bundle of letters toward her.

The envelopes were yellowed with age and tied together with a thin red ribbon. DJ looked at her cousin as she picked them up with trembling fingers. "They must have meant something to your grandmother for her to keep them like this."

Dana nodded. "I thought the same thing. I can't imagine turning my back on my children, no matter what they did."

"You haven't met my father," she said with a sad smile. "I'm sure he sounded charming on the phone. But he was a born con man. He never did an honest day's work in his life. That's how he ended up in prison."

"My grandparents were hardworking ranchers, up before dawn, so they must have been horribly disappointed that their only son wasn't interested in staying on the ranch," Dana said with such diplomacy that DJ loved her all the more for it.

"You don't mind if I open these and read them?" she asked.

"Of course not. They're from your father. If they can help, please. I just don't want them to upset you."

DJ laughed, thinking of all the things she'd been through tonight, Beau being one of them. "I was raised by my father. Nothing about him would surprise me." She knew that wasn't quite true. When he'd mentioned Montana, what she'd heard in his voice—longing, regret, love—*that* had surprised her.

She opened the first letter. Something about her father's precise handwriting made her ache inside. It was clear even before she read the first few words that he was trying hard to make amends. He wanted his parents to get to know his wife.

DJ put that letter away and picked up another. This one was along the same lines as the first. He talked about wanting to return to the ranch, to raise a family there.

The next letter was even more heartbreaking. He was pleading with his parents to forgive him. She saw that the letters had been written only weeks apart.

DJ wasn't sure she could read the last letter. The writing was so neat, so purposeful, so pleading. In this letter, he said that he desperately wanted his family to meet his baby girl, DJ.

Don't punish her for my mistakes. Please don't deny your grandchild because of mistakes I've made. I will do anything you ask of me. I'll do it for my child… I'd do anything for DJ. All she has is me.

As she read the last lines, her eyes burned with tears, the words blurring before her. She quickly closed the letter and put it back into the envelope. He had pleaded for their forgiveness and asked if he and his baby could come home. Clearly they hadn't forgiven him, since her cousin had never met him.

But she and her father must have come to Montana later, when she was five. How else could she have met ten-year-old Beau Tanner? How else could her father have forced such a promise out of him?

He'd tried to give her family. She didn't think his words could break her heart any further and yet they had. He'd poured his heart out to his parents and yet they hadn't budged. No wonder he'd never told her about his family. But what had he done to make them so cold to him?

"He must have done something they felt was unforgivable. I can't believe it was simply for marrying a woman of Italian descent," she said and looked at her cousin.

"I don't know. I never really knew my grandparents. I was young when they died, but they were very strict, from what my mother told me. However, I'm with you.

I don't think it was the marriage. I think something else happened. Maybe if you asked your father—"

"He isn't apt to tell me, unfortunately, since I knew nothing about any of this," she said quickly and got to her feet. "There is something I'd like to show you." She picked up her bag from the chair where she'd dropped it. "Do you recognize this?" she asked as she held out the doll to her cousin.

Dana took the rag doll so carefully, holding it gingerly as she looked into its innocent face. "It's old, isn't it? Was it yours when you were a child?" she asked as she studied the construction and clothing.

"You've never seen it before?"

"No, I'm sorry. I can tell that it is handmade." She pointed to the small embroidered red heart, almost like a birthmark, on the doll's chest, under the collar of her dress. "Did someone make the doll for you?"

"That's what's so…frustrating. I had an identical doll, but I lost it years ago. When I first saw this one, I thought it was mine. It's not, though. Mine had an accident with a dog."

"How odd. So, how did you come to have this one?" Dana asked.

"I recently found it in my bed in my apartment."

Her cousin quickly rubbed her arms as if chilled. "That is spooky. And you have no idea who could have left it for you?"

She shook her head. "None. But this was pinned to the rag doll's body, under her dress." She took out the photo and handed it to her cousin. "What about the people in this photograph? Do you recognize them?" DJ asked hopefully.

Dana studied the old photograph for a long moment before shaking her head. "I'm sorry, but I've never seen them before."

Taking the photo back, she felt a deep sense of disappointment. She'd hoped that her cousin would have the answers she desperately needed.

On the table was one of the first letters she'd opened. "Did you see this part?" she asked her cousin. "There was another woman my father had been in love with that summer. Apparently it was someone his parents adored. If he broke that woman's heart…" She looked back through the letter. "He mentions a Zinnie." Glancing up at Dana, she asked, "Do you know anyone by that name?"

Her cousin thought for a moment. "Could be Zinnia Jameson. Well, at least, that's her name now. She married a local rancher. She would be about the right age. They live about ten miles up the canyon. It's too late to ask her tonight."

"But we could go tomorrow?"

Dana smiled and rose. "Tomorrow, though if your father broke her heart, she might not want to talk about it."

"It was more than thirty-five years ago."

"As if that makes a difference when it comes to

a broken heart," her cousin said. "Maybe Zinnia is why Walter's parents couldn't forgive him."

ROGER DOUGLAS HAD just poured himself a drink when his phone rang. He couldn't help being nervous. If he didn't get rid of Dee Anna Justice... Paying her off wasn't an option. That would mean opening up the financials. He couldn't let that happen. All he needed was a little more time to win the money back. There was a poker game tomorrow night. High stakes. With a little luck...

The phone rang again. He pulled it out of his pocket, expecting it would be Marietta. He really wasn't in the mood to talk to her tonight.

With surprise, he saw that it was the man he'd hired to find him a killer. Was he calling to say the deed was done? His heart soared. With Dee Anna Justice dead, he would have the time he desperately needed to cover his tracks.

"Tell me you have good news," he said into the phone without preamble.

"We have a problem."

"I don't want to hear—"

"He thinks you put an earlier hit out on her."

"What? That's ridiculous."

"Well, something's wrong. He says there's this cowboy dogging her like he thinks someone is going to try to kill her."

"I have no idea what that's about, let alone who

this cowboy might be. You said that other man you talked to about this…contract could be a problem."

"It's not him."

"You sure about that?"

"Look, I'll talk Andrei down. He's a pro. He'll complete the contract."

"What about the other guy?"

"Jimmy? Who knows? He might get lucky and take her out. He's cheaper, and with the pro getting cold feet, this could work out better for both of us."

"It had better."

"Easy, Roger. The only reason you and I are pals is that you owe my boss a potful of money. So remember who you're talking to." He hung up.

Roger downed his drink and poured himself another. If this blew up in his face…

BEAU WOULDN'T HAVE been surprised to find his house empty when he finally got home. Leah had shown up like a ghost out of the past. He half expected her to vanish the same way.

The house was dark as he entered. As he turned on the light, he was startled for a moment to see a shadowy figure sitting by the window.

"You could have turned on a light," he said, annoyed with her for showing up, for only hinting at whatever was wrong and now for startling him.

"I like the dark," she said, turning to look at him.

"Also, you can't see the northern lights with a lamp on. Didn't you notice them?"

He hadn't. He'd had too much on his mind.

"Rough night?" she asked as he hung up his Stetson and coat.

"You could say that. Look, I'm not staying, so now probably isn't the best time for you to tell me what's going on with you and Charlie."

She nodded, making him wonder if she was ever going to tell him. "Is everything all right?"

"Just work."

Leah nodded as if to say she knew he was putting her off and it was okay. She got up and followed him into the kitchen. In the overhead light, he could see that she'd been crying.

"Once I finish this job—"

"It's all right. But I do appreciate you letting me stay here."

He nodded as he made himself two sandwiches and bagged them with a couple of colas. "I'm going to grab a quick shower."

"I was just headed for bed. I didn't realize how late it was. Beau, if there is anything I can do—"

"No. Thanks for cleaning up after yourself."

She laughed. "I didn't mean in the house. I have some experience with undercover operations."

He stared at her. "As what?"

"An operative. But we can talk about that when this job of yours is over."

An operative? He realized how little he knew about her and Charlie as he watched her head for the guest bedroom. He'd thought that she and his former best friend were having marital problems. Now he didn't know what to think.

He didn't have time to speculate. Right now, his number one problem was DJ Justice.

Chapter Nine

It was after midnight. The snow-covered mountain-side shone like day in the light of the huge white moon hanging overhead.

"Let me walk you to your cabin," Dana said as DJ started to leave.

"No, it's late and I can get there just fine on my own." She smiled at her cousin and gave her a hug. "But thank you. For everything."

"I'm sorry I wasn't more help with the doll and photo. Tomorrow, though, we'll pay Zinnia a visit."

"We'll get it figured out," DJ said, hoping it was true. At least she knew more now than she had before coming here. Her father's letters still broke her heart. What had he done?

"So you liked Beau?" Dana asked almost shyly.

DJ chuckled and shook her head. "The truth is, my father asked him to look after me while I'm out here."

"Really? What did he think might happen to you? Or," she said, smiling, "was he trying to throw the two of you together?" From the glint in her cousin's eyes, it was clear that she thought Walter was also playing matchmaker.

DJ shrugged. She really had no idea. If she hadn't seen her father's fear… "Again, thank you for everything. See you in the morning." As DJ stepped out on the porch, closing the door behind her, she caught movement out of the corner of her eye. For a startled moment, her hand went to her bag. Unfortunately she'd had to leave her gun behind in California.

Beau Tanner rose from the chair he'd been sprawled in, his boots scraping the wood porch as he tipped his Stetson. "Didn't mean to scare you."

"What are you doing here?" He *had* scared her, but she was trying hard not to show it.

"My job. I told you. Your father—"

"And I told you. I can take care of myself. I release you from any promise you made when you were ten." She started off the porch but heard his boots right behind her. She spun on him. "What are you planning to do? Follow me everywhere?"

"If that's what it takes to make sure you're safe."

She thrust her hands on her hips. "This is crazy. Look, I'm fine. There is nothing to protect me from."

"You sure about that? Well, I'm not. And until I am…"

"Fine. Follow me if it makes you happy." She started up the mountainside, breathing hard from her anger and just seeing him again. The last thing she needed right now was some man who…who irritated her. Her heart was beating faster at just the sound of his long strides as he easily caught up to her.

"Let's just keep to the shadows of the pines," he said, pulling her out of the moonlight.

She indulged him and his paranoia, filling her lungs with the cold night air as she tried to ignore him. The cowboy wasn't the kind who was easily ignored. She caught a whiff of his scent, a mixture of the great outdoors, fragrant soap and a powerful maleness.

DJ hated the effect it had on her as her body betrayed her. She felt an ache inside her like something she'd never felt before. Maybe it was from years of not feeling safe, but she wanted to be in his arms again. She wanted to feel again like she had that moment in the snowbank when his mouth was on hers. She wanted to feel…protected, and she had in his arms.

Which was why she couldn't let herself give in. She would be here only a few days, and then she would be returning to California and her life there.

"This is where we part company," she said as she climbed the steps to her cabin and started to open the door.

He'd taken the steps in long strides, and now his large hand closed over hers. "Not until I make sure the cabin is secure."

She opened the door, turning on the light as she

stepped inside, Beau right behind her. She couldn't believe how far he was taking this. "It's late and I need to get some rest."

He didn't seem to be paying any attention to what she was saying. She hadn't wanted him in her cabin. Earlier the place had felt spacious, but it didn't now. "This is silly. You can see that there is no one in here."

He turned to look at her. "I think you have some idea who might want to harm you. That's information I need. Tonight. Before this goes any further."

She heard the determination in his voice and sighed inwardly. *Let him have his say and then send him on his way*, she thought. "Fine."

It had been a long day, but after the nap earlier and everything that had happened, she felt more wired than tired, in truth. She moved to the small kitchen and opened the refrigerator, remembering the variety of beverages and snacks her cousin had shown her.

"Wine or beer?" she asked, knowing the only reason she was asking was that she needed the distraction.

"Beer." He had moved to the small breakfast bar and taken a seat on one of the stools. She handed him a bottle of beer and took one for herself. Twisting off the top, she took a drink. It was icy cold and tasted good.

Leaning against the kitchen counter, she studied the handsome cowboy. It was his eyes, she thought.

She had remembered them because they were so un-usual. Worn denim. Maybe also because there was kindness in those eyes that she would have recognized even as a child of five.

"I'm sorry you got involved in this," she said as she picked at the label on her bottle for a moment. When she looked up, she realized he'd been studying *her.*

"WHY DOES YOUR father think you need protecting?" Beau asked and watched her take another drink of her beer as if stalling. He understood she was holding out on him. He'd been in this business long enough to know the signs. DJ was running scared, but she was trying damned hard not to show it.

"You say you met me years ago?" she finally asked. "Did you know anything about my family before that? Or after that?"

He had removed his Stetson and tossed it on one of the other stools. Now he shrugged out of his coat, the same one he'd worn to the airport. He could see that this was going to take a while.

"Are you going somewhere with these questions? Or just avoiding mine?" he asked after draping his coat over a stool. He locked gazes with her. "I have to wonder why you aren't being straight with me. I hate getting myself killed without knowing why."

She looked chagrined as she put down her beer and turned to him. "I'm not sure what this has to do with anything, but before I left California, my apartment was broken into. The intruder left something for me."

He held his breath as he waited, imagining all kinds of nasty things.

"It was a doll with a photo pinned to it." She nodded as if she could tell that wasn't what he'd expected. "I used to have a rag doll identical to it. It wasn't a commercial doll. Someone had made it. Made two, apparently. Because as it turns out, this one wasn't mine. But it is so much like mine…"

"…that you wondered whose it had been."

She smiled. "Glad you're following along."

"And the photo?"

She reached into her shoulder bag and took out the doll and photo. She handed him the photo. "I don't recognize any of them or have any idea who they might be. I asked my father, but…"

"He said he didn't know them."

"But from his expression when he saw the photo, he knows who they are. He suggested I get out of town."

Beau studied the photo. "You think you might be this baby?"

"My father swore I wasn't."

"But you don't believe him."

She sighed. "I don't know what to believe. For years he told me I had no family. A couple of days ago I find out about the Cardwells—and the Justices.

My father was born here, apparently. His family disowned him after he married my mother. He wrote a few letters trying to get back into their good graces. He must even have come here if you and I met all those years ago."

"You think he was here trying to make amends?"

"It doesn't sound like making amends was the only reason my father came here. Otherwise I doubt we would have met."

Beau nodded as he picked up the doll she'd set on the breakfast bar. "I called your father after I saw you at the airport today."

That surprised her. She took a drink of her beer and seemed to be waiting for what was coming.

"I told him that in order to protect you, I needed to know what I was protecting you from," he said. "Your father swore that he didn't know, but when I pressed him, he said it might have something to do with your mother's family. He said they might have…found you."

She shuddered. *"Found me?"*

"That's what *I* said. Unfortunately he had to go before he could tell me anything further. I thought you might know why he would say that."

DJ stepped past him to move to the window that looked out over the ranch. As she drew back the curtain, he said, "I wish you wouldn't do that."

She let the curtain fall into place and turned to look at him. "You think this has something to do with my *mother's* family? Why would they leave me the doll and the photo if they didn't want me to know about them?"

"Maybe they didn't leave them. Maybe some well-meaning person did." He shrugged. "I got the impression that your father thought you had something to fear from them."

She took another sip of her beer. "Well, that's interesting, given that all my life he's told me I didn't have any family. Not just that," she said as she walked back to the counter where she'd been leaning earlier. "I always felt growing up that we were running from something, someone. A few times it was one of my father's…associates. But other times…"

"You think it might have been your mother's family?"

She shrugged and toyed with the label on her beer again. He saw her eyes fill with tears. "That would be something, if the people I have to fear are…family."

"We don't know that." He got up, moved to her and took the nearly full bottle of beer from her. He set it aside. "You should get some rest."

He expected her to put up a fight, but instead she merely nodded. "It has been a long day." Her gaze met his. He did his best not to look at her full mouth.

Stepping away from her, he reached for his coat and hat.

"As it turns out, my father had a girlfriend before he married my mother," she said behind him.

"Dana and I are going to visit a woman named Zinnia in the morning. I have a bad feeling he broke her heart. Still, I'm hoping she might be able to help me put another piece into the puzzle that is my father."

"I'm going, too, then."

"I told you. I release you from any promise you made my father years ago."

He nodded as he shrugged into his coat. "Just the same, I can go with you or follow you. Your choice." Beau snugged his Stetson down over his blond hair. His boots echoed on the hardwood floor as he walked to the door, opened it and turned. "I'll be right outside if you need me." He tipped his hat to her.

She opened her mouth, no doubt to argue the point, but he was out the door before she could speak. As he settled into the swing on the porch, he listened to her moving around inside the cabin and tried not to think of her in that big log bed he'd seen through the open bedroom doorway.

"STACY? DID I wake you?" Jimmy knocked over the bottle of whiskey, swore and grabbed it before most of it ended up in the motel carpet. "You still there?"

"Jimmy?" she said sleepily.

"James. I told you, I go by James now." He took a drink and pushed aside his irritation at her. Tonight hadn't gone as he'd planned, and he felt the clock ticking. Who knew what the pro was doing tonight, but getting into the ranch wouldn't be easy for him—

especially at night. There were hired hands, ranch dogs, lots of people living there. Unless they knew you... He told himself he still had the upper hand.

"What do you want?" Stacy asked, sounding irritated with him now.

He quieted his voice. "I was thinking about you. Thinking about old times. You and me." He could almost feel her soften at his words. Whatever he had back then, he still had it—at least where Stacy was concerned.

"So you decided to call me in the middle of the night?" She didn't sound irritated anymore. Maybe she was a little touched by the gesture.

"Yeah, sorry about that. I just couldn't get you off my mind. I wanted to hear your voice."

"You didn't say what you were doing in town. Are you living here now?"

He'd been vague, letting her think he was looking for a job, a place to live, letting her think he might be staying. "We can talk about that sometime, but right now I want to talk about you."

"What about me?"

"I still remember the way you felt in my arms."

"You do?"

"Uh-huh. Do you remember...me?"

She made an affirming sound.

He could imagine her lying in bed. He wondered what she had on. Probably a flannel nightgown, but he could get that off her quick enough.

"You are the sexiest woman I've ever known," he said and took another sip of the whiskey. "You said you live on the ranch now. In one of those cabins on the mountainside that I can see from the road?"

"Jim—James."

"I was thinking maybe—"

"My daughter. Ella, I told you about her. She's here in the cabin with me."

"I would be quiet as a mouse." There was just enough hesitation that it gave him hope, but she quickly drowned that idea.

"No. If that's all you wanted, I really need to get some sleep."

He realized that he'd come on too strong. He cursed under his breath. "No, that's not all I want. I shouldn't have called tonight. But after seeing you... I want to take you out to a nice dinner. That is, if you're free."

Silence, then, "When?"

"Tomorrow night. I figure you'll know a good place to go. Nothing cheap. I want to make up for this call."

"Okay."

He shot a fist into the air. "Great. I'll pick you up. What time? And hey, I want to meet your daughter." He'd almost forgotten about the kid again.

"Sure," she said, sounding pleased. "Tomorrow, say, six? My sister will babysit Ella."

"See if she'll take her for the night, because I want

to get you on a dance floor after dinner. I can't wait to get you in my arms again."

Stacy laughed. "I've missed you."

He smiled to himself as he hung up and picked up the hunting knife from the bed. "Tomorrow night." He would mix a little pleasure with business.

Chapter Ten

The next morning, just after sunrise, Dana found Beau on DJ's porch. She handed him a mug of coffee and a key. "Go over to the cabin next door. I can stand guard if you think it's necessary."

He smiled at her, glad to have Dana for a friend. "I don't think you need to stand guard." He figured DJ should be safe in broad daylight with so many people on the ranch. And he didn't plan on being gone long.

"Thanks for the coffee—and the key. But I think I'll run home and get a shower and a change of clothing. DJ said the two of you are going to visit Zinnia Jameson. I'd like to come along."

"Fine with me. I'm glad you're looking after her." Her smile seemed to hold a tiny surprise. "She's special, don't you think?"

He laughed. "You're barking up the wrong tree. It isn't like that." He thought about the kiss and quickly shoved the memory away.

"That's what they all say—until love hits them like a ton of bricks."

Beau left, chuckling to himself. He'd heard that Dana Savage was one great matchmaker. She'd helped all five of her cousins find the loves of their lives. But she'd apparently failed with her older sister, Stacy, he thought.

And she would fail with him.

On the way home, Beau put in another call to the number Walter Justice had given him. A male voice answered just as before. He asked for Walter Justice.

A moment later another male voice came on the line. The gravelly voice informed him that Walter couldn't come to the phone.

"I need to talk to him."

"Not sure if that is ever going to happen. He got shanked last night. They've taken him to the hospital."

"Is he going to be all right?"

"Don't know." The line went dead.

Beau held his phone for a few moments, listening to the silence on the other end. DJ's father was in the hospital, possibly dying? There might never be any answers coming from that end.

He pocketed his phone, telling himself that he needed to let DJ know. She said she didn't care about her father, but having been through this with his own, he knew it wasn't true. When the man was your father, no matter how much he screwed up, his loss…well, it hurt. He remembered feeling racked with guilt because he hadn't kept in touch with his father. For years he'd wanted nothing to do with him.

Ultimately it all came down to blood and a built-in love that came with it.

Reaching his house, he climbed out of his pickup, thinking about the Walter Justice he'd known years ago. He wondered how he'd aged since he'd been in prison. He doubted he'd changed, which could explain why he was in the hospital now.

Beau swore under his breath. He didn't know what to do. He had to keep DJ safe. It was a debt that he wouldn't renege on—even if Walter didn't survive. He wasn't the kind of man who went back on his word. But he also knew there was more to it. He kept thinking about that brown-eyed little girl and the woman she'd become.

He would tell her about her father. But not until after their visit to Zinnia Jameson's house. He wasn't sure how she would take the news. Maybe there was no connection between what had happened to her father and whatever Walter feared might happen to his daughter.

Either way, Beau was even more concerned for her safety.

ANDREI SNIFFED THE WIND, waiting for a sign. He clung to the utility pole, careful not to attract any undue attention.

This job had turned out to be harder than he'd

thought. For some reason Dee Anna had picked up an overprotective cowboy. Because of that, he was having trouble getting the right shot.

That alone should have made him quit the job.

But his birthday was coming, and he'd planned this for too long. His last hit. He would feel incomplete if he didn't finish. Also, he never quit a job once he'd flipped the coin and it had come up heads. It felt like a bad idea to do it now. He never liked to test luck.

So he would finish it and celebrate his birthday as he hung up his gun.

All he had to do was kill Dee Anna Justice. But not today, he thought as he sniffed the wind again. She and the cowboy had to feel safe. Then they would make the mistake of letting him get a clean shot. He would bide his time.

"THIS COULDN'T WAIT until a decent time of the day?" attorney Roger Douglas demanded as he joined Marietta in the library. He stepped to the table where Ester had put out coffee and mini citrus muffins. He poured himself a cup and took two muffins on a small plate before sitting down.

"I wanted an update on the…situation," Marietta said. She felt calm and in control, more than she had in the few months since Carlotta had confessed.

"It's a little early to—"

"I assumed you would be handling this yourself and yet here you sit."

He picked up one of the muffins. She noticed that his hand shook as he popped it into his mouth. Clearly he was stalling for time.

"Have you even found her?" she demanded.

"Yes, of course. She's at a place called the Cardwell Ranch near Big Sky, Montana. She's staying with a cousin on her father's side of the family. I've had her apartment bugged for several months—ever since you asked me to find her."

"But you haven't gotten around to offering her money?"

"What is this really about?" Roger asked patiently, as if she was a child he had to humor.

"Have you offered Dee Anna Justice the money or not?"

He studied her for a moment before dragging his gaze away. "Maybe we should discuss this when you are more yourself."

"Actually, I am, and for the first time in a long time. I am going to want to see all the financials on the trust funds." He paled, confirming what she'd feared. Her nosy housekeeper knew more than she did about what was right in front of her eyes. "But on this other matter…"

Roger rose. "I don't know what's gotten into you, but I told you I would handle it."

"How much are you planning to offer her?" She

saw something in his eyes that made her heart drop. How much money had he stolen from her? Was this why he was dragging his feet? Because there wasn't enough money left to bribe Dee Anna Justice?

"What did you do?" she demanded.

He began to pace the room. "You're not thinking clearly, so I had to take things into my own hands. Trying to buy off this woman is the wrong approach. She would eventually bleed you dry. You know what kind of woman she is given that her father is Walter Justice. I told you I'm taking care of it and I have. I've hired someone to make sure she is no longer a problem."

For a moment Marietta couldn't catch her breath. "You did what?"

He dropped down into a chair next to her and took one of her hands. "It is the only way. I've kept you out of it. I—"

She jerked her hand free. "You stupid fool." Her mind raced. "Is it done already?"

"No, but I should be hearing from him—"

"Stop him!" She shoved to her feet. She was breathing hard, her heart thumping crazily in her chest. She tried to calm down. If she had a heart attack now... "You stop him or I will call the police."

Roger looked too shocked to speak. "You wouldn't do that."

"Try me. Call him now!"

"My job is to protect you."

She shook her head. "Protect me? Give me your phone. I will stop the man myself." She held out her hand.

"You can't do that, Marietta." He sounded scared. "You don't know what this man is capable of doing if he feels you're jerking him around."

"You think he is more dangerous than me?" She let out a chuckle, feeling stronger than she had in years. "Roger, get your affairs in order. You're done, and if I find out what I suspect, that you've been stealing from me, prepare for spending the rest of your life in prison. You're fired, and if you try to run, I'll send this man after you."

All the color had drained from his face. "You don't know what you're saying."

"I do, for the first time in a long time. I've depended on you to make decisions for me because you made me question myself. But I'm clearheaded now, Roger." He started to argue, but she cut him off. "Make the call."

She watched, shaking inside. But whoever he was phoning didn't answer. She listened to him leave a message calling off the hit.

"This is a mistake," Roger said as he pocketed his phone. "I've been with you for years. I've—"

"Get out." She pointed toward the door. "Don't make me call the police to have you thrown out. And you'd better pray that the man you hired gets the message."

As he left, Marietta heard a floorboard creak. Ester. The nosy damned woman. She thought about firing her as well, but she was too upset to deal with another traitor in her midst right now.

THE WOMAN WHO answered the door later that morning at the Jameson house was tiny, with a halo of white-blond hair that framed a gentle face. Bright blue eyes peered out at them from behind wire-rimmed glasses. "Yes?" she asked, looking from DJ to Beau and finally to Dana. She brightened when she recognized her.

"Sorry to drop by without calling," Dana said.

"No, I'm delighted." She stepped back to let them enter.

"This is my cousin DJ."

"Dee Anna Justice," DJ added, watching the woman for a reaction to the last name. She didn't have to wait long.

Zinnia froze for a moment before her gaze shot to DJ, her blue eyes widening. "Wally's daughter?"

DJ nodded. She'd never heard anyone call her father Wally.

"And you know Beau Tanner," Dana said.

"Yes," Zinnia said. An awkward silence fell between them, but she quickly filled it. "I was just going to put on a pot of coffee. Come into the kitchen, where we can visit while I make it." Her eyes hadn't left DJ's face.

They followed her into the kitchen. DJ had been so nervous all morning, afraid that this might be another dead end. But now, from Zinnia's reaction to her, she had little doubt this woman had been the one her father's parents had hoped he would marry.

"Dana is helping me piece together my past—and my father's," DJ said, unable to wait a moment longer. "You were a part of the past, if I'm not wrong."

Zinnia had her back to them. She stopped pouring coffee grounds into a white paper filter for a moment. "Yes." She finished putting the coffee on and turned. "Please sit."

DJ pulled out a chair at the table. Her cousin did the same across from her. Beau stood by the window.

Zinnia came around the kitchen island to pull up a chair at the head of the table. When she looked at DJ, her expression softened. "I loved your father. Is that what you wanted to hear?"

"And he loved you."

The woman nodded, a faraway look in those blue eyes. "We'd been in love since grade school." She chuckled. "I know that sounds silly, but it's true. We were inseparable. We even attended Montana State University in Bozeman together. Everyone just assumed we would get married after college."

"Especially my father's parents," DJ said.

"Yes. I had a very good relationship with them. I was like another daughter to them, they said." She smiled in memory.

"What happened?" DJ asked, even though she suspected she already knew.

Zinnia straightened in her chair as if bracing herself. "Wally got a job as a wrangler taking people into Yellowstone Park. His parents were upset with him because they needed him on the ranch, but Wally was restless. He'd already confessed to me that he didn't want to take over the ranch when his parents retired. He wanted to travel. He wanted…" She hesitated. "That's just it. He didn't know what he wanted. He just…*wanted*." Her gaze locked on DJ's. "Then he met your mother. She and some friends were touring the park." Zinnia shrugged, but her voice cracked when she added, "Apparently it was love at first sight."

The coffeemaker let out a sigh, and the woman got up.

DJ rose, too. "May I help?"

Zinnia seemed surprised. "Why, thank you. There are cups in that cabinet."

She took out four cups and watched as Zinnia filled each. DJ carried two over, giving one to Dana and the other to Beau as he finally took a seat at the table. She'd expected to see him on her front porch when she got up this morning, but to her surprise, he'd come driving up, all showered and shaved and ready to go wherever she was going.

He'd been so somber, she wondered if he wasn't having second thoughts about getting involved with her father—and her. She couldn't blame him. It seemed ridiculous for him to tag along, since she seemed to be in no danger. Maybe her father had overreacted.

She'd said as much to Beau, but he'd insisted that he had nothing else planned that day except spend it with her.

Because of some promise he'd made a con man when he was ten? What kind of man would honor that?

Beau Tanner, she thought, turning her attention back to Zinnia.

"My grandparents must have been horribly disappointed," DJ said after taking the cup of coffee the woman handed her and sitting back down.

Zinnia sat, cradling her cup in her two small hands. "They were as brokenhearted as I was," she said with a nod and then took a sip of her coffee, her eyes misty.

DJ wanted to tell her that she'd dodged a bullet by not ending up with her father. But even as she thought it, she wondered what kind of man her father might have been if he'd married Zinnia and gotten over his wanderlust.

"I had no idea that my mother had a brother," Dana said into the awkward silence. "Then I found some old letters. That's how we found you."

Zinnia nodded. "Wally's parents did everything they could to get him not to marry that girl, to come back to the ranch, to help them, since they were getting up in age. Mostly they wanted him to marry me." She smiled sadly. "But in the end..." Her voice broke. "Sadly, I heard the marriage didn't last long." Her gaze was on DJ again.

"My mother died in childbirth."

The older woman seemed startled to hear that.

DJ stared at her. "That is what happened, right?"

"I only know what Wally's parents told me."

"It would help if you could tell us what you do know," Dana said.

Zinnia hesitated for a moment and then spoke quietly. "As you might have guessed, I stayed friends with Wally's parents. They were such sweet people. They were devastated when Wally didn't come back." She took a sip of her coffee as if gathering her thoughts. "Wally called at one point, asking for money. I guess he thought they would give him what he felt was his share of the ranch." She scoffed at that. "He always made things worse."

Seeming to realize that she was talking about DJ's father, Zinnia quickly added, "Forgive me for talking about him like that."

"There isn't anything you can say that I haven't said myself. I know my father. He didn't get better after he left Montana."

"Well," the older woman continued. "When he called for money, he told them that Carlotta—" the name seemed to cause her pain even after all these years "—had left him to go spend time with an aunt in Italy."

DJ reached into her shoulder bag and took out the photo. As she passed it over to Zinnia, she asked, "Do you recognize any of these people?"

Zinnia studied the photo for only a moment before she put it down. "The young woman holding the baby is Carlotta Pisani Justice. Or at least, that had been her name. I saw her only once, but that's definitely her. You can see why Wally fell for her."

Picking up the photograph, DJ stared at the young woman holding the baby. This was her *mother*. "My father swears that the baby she's holding isn't me."

Zinnia looked at her with sympathy. "We heard that her wealthy family had gotten the marriage annulled somehow and threatened that if she didn't go to Italy, they would cut off her money. It seems she met someone her family liked better in Italy, quickly remarried and had a child with him."

"So this child would be my half brother or sister," DJ said more to herself. When she looked up, she saw Zinnia's expression.

The older woman was frowning. "But if her family had the marriage annulled… Why would they have done that after your mother and father had a child together?"

DJ felt an odd buzzing in her ears. She thought about what Beau had told her. Her father feared that her mother's family had "found" her.

"Is it possible they didn't know about me?" DJ asked, finding herself close to tears. Her gaze went to Beau's. She saw sympathy in his gaze but not surprise. All those years on the run. Had they been running to keep the truth from her mother's family?

The doll and the photo meant *someone* knew about her. Not only that, they also wanted her to know about them.

BEAU DROVE DJ and Dana back to the ranch after their visit with Zinnia. Both were quiet on the short drive. The sun had come out, making the snowy landscape sparkle like diamonds. As he drove, he chewed on what they'd learned from Zinnia. He felt for DJ. Apparently her mother had walked away not only from her father but also from her.

But what part had her father played? He could only guess.

He hated that the news he had to give her would only make her feel worse. But he had no choice. He couldn't keep something like this from her. She had to know.

As he pulled into the Cardwell Ranch and parked, Dana's children all came running out. They were begging to go see Santa at the mall in Bozeman.

Stacy was with them. "I didn't put it in their heads," she said quickly.

Dana laughed. "Looks like I'm going to the mall,"

FREE Merchandise and a Cash Reward† are 'in the Cards' for you!

Dear Reader,

We're giving away FREE MERCHANDISE and a CASH REWARD!

Seriously, we'd like to reward you for reading this novel by giving you **FREE MERCHANDISE** worth over $20 retail plus a CASH REWARD! And no purchase is necessary!

You see the Jack of Hearts sticker above? Paste that sticker in the box on the Free Merchandise Voucher inside. Return the Voucher today… and we'll send you Free Merchandise plus a Cash Reward!

Thanks again for reading one of our novels—and enjoy your Free Merchandise and Cash Reward with our compliments!

Pam Powers

Pam Powers

P.S. Look inside to see what Free Merchandise is **"in the cards"** for you!

We'd like to send you two free books like the one you are enjoying now. Your two books have a combined price of over $10 retail, but they are yours to keep absolutely FREE! We'll even send you 2 wonderful surprise gifts and a Cash Reward†. You can't lose!

REMEMBER: Your Free Merchandise, consisting of **2 Free Books** and **2 Free Gifts**, is worth over $20 retail! Plus we'll send you a **Cash Reward** (it's a dollar) which is really the icing on the cake because it's in addition to your FREE Merchandise! No purchase is necessary, so please send for your Free Merchandise today.

Get TWO FREE GIFTS!

We'll also send you 2 wonderful FREE GIFTS (worth about $10 retail), in addition to your 2 Free books and Cash Reward!

Visit us at:
www.ReaderService.com

YOUR FREE MERCHANDISE INCLUDES...
2 FREE Books **AND** 2 FREE Mystery Gifts
PLUS you'll get a Cash Reward†

▶ Detach card and mail today. No stamp needed. ▶

FREE MERCHANDISE VOUCHER

2 FREE BOOKS and **2 FREE GIFTS**

Please send my Free Merchandise, consisting of
2 Free Books and **2 Free Mystery Gifts** PLUS my
Cash Reward. I understand that I am under no
obligation to buy anything, as explained
on the back of this card.

❏ I prefer the regular-print edition
182/382 HDL GLVA

❏ I prefer the larger-print edition
199/399 HDL GLVA

Please Print

| |
| |

FIRST NAME

| |
| |

LAST NAME

| |
| |

ADDRESS

| | |
| | |

APT.#   CITY

| | |
| | |

STATE/PROV.   ZIP/POSTAL CODE

Offer limited to one per household and not applicable to series that subscriber is currently receiving.
Your Privacy—The Reader Service is committed to protecting your privacy. Our Privacy Policy is available online at www.ReaderService.com or upon request from the Reader Service. We make a portion of our mailing list available to reputable third parties that offer products we believe may interest you. If you prefer that we not exchange your name with third parties, or if you wish to clarify or modify your communication preferences, please visit us at www.ReaderService.com/consumerschoice or write to us at Reader Service Preference Service, P.O. Box 9062, Buffalo, NY 14240-9062. Include your complete name and address.

NO PURCHASE NECESSARY!

I-N16-FMC15

BUSINESS REPLY MAIL

FIRST-CLASS MAIL   PERMIT NO. 717   BUFFALO, NY

POSTAGE WILL BE PAID BY ADDRESSEE

READER SERVICE
PO BOX 1867
BUFFALO NY 14240-9952

NO POSTAGE
NECESSARY
IF MAILED
IN THE
UNITED STATES

she said as she started toward the kids. "DJ, you're welcome to come along. You, too, Beau."

Beau shook his head. "Thanks, but DJ and I have some things we need to iron out."

Dana shot her cousin a mischievous look.

"Tell Santa hello for me," DJ said.

Beau said to Dana, "Mind if we take a couple of horses for a ride?"

Dana grinned. "Please. I'll call down to the stables. DJ, you can wear what you wore last night. You'll find a warmer coat just inside the door of the house."

"You do ride, don't you?" he asked her.

"I've been on a horse, if that's what you mean. But whatever you have to tell me, you don't have to take me for a ride to do it."

A man came out of the house just then, wearing a marshal's uniform. Dana introduced them. DJ could tell that something was worrying him and feared it might have to do with her.

"Have you had any trouble with the electricity?" he asked Dana.

"No, why?"

"Burt came by with the mail and told me he'd seen a lineman on one of our poles. By the time I got here, he was gone. Just thought I'd ask. Burt's pretty protective, but still, it did seem odd. Maybe I'll give the power company a call."

As Hud drove away, followed by Stacy and Dana

and the kids, DJ turned to Beau. "Seriously, we can't talk here?"

He smiled and shook his head. "Let's get saddled up. We can talk about who's taking whom for a ride once we're on horseback and high in the mountains."

"I'm not going to like whatever it is you need to tell me, am I?"

He shook his head. "No, you're not, but you need to hear it."

WHEN HE'D SEEN Dee Anna and her cowboy saddling up horses, Andrei had known this was the day. Several things had happened that he'd taken as signs. He would have good luck today.

He'd made arrangements the night before to procure a snowmobile. He'd been stealing since he was a boy and still got a thrill out of it. He'd always liked the danger—and the reward. His father had taught him how to get away with it. He smiled to himself at the memory. He missed his father and hoped that he would make him proud today.

Andrei felt good. He was going to get his chance to finish this. He didn't plan to kill the cowboy, too, but he would if he had to. He could tell that the two felt safe here on the ranch. As they rode toward the mountains behind the ranch house, he smiled to himself.

Today would definitely be the day. Last night after stealing the snowmobile, he'd traversed the logging roads behind the ranch. He would be waiting for them on the mountain. He had an idea where they would be riding to. He'd seen horse tracks at a spot where there was a view of the tiny resort town of Big Sky.

He would be waiting for them. One shot. That's all he needed. He would be ahead of schedule. Still, he wanted to get this over with. He knew that feeling wasn't conducive to the type of work that he did. But he couldn't help the way he felt. He was anxious. Once he finished this, he couldn't wait for the future he'd planned since his first job when he was fourteen.

His cell phone rang. He ignored it. He could almost taste success on the wind as he climbed on the snowmobile and headed up one of the logging roads toward the top of the mountain behind Cardwell Ranch.

FROM THE WINDOW Marietta watched her granddaughter come up the circular drive and park the little red sports car that had been her present for her thirtieth birthday.

"She can buy her own car," Ester had said with disapproval. "She has a job. It would be good for her and mean more to her."

Marietta had scoffed at that. "I have no one else to spoil." Which was true—at least, she'd believed that Bianca was her only granddaughter at the time. "She is my blood." Blood meant everything in her family. It was where lines were drawn. It was what made Bianca so precious. She was her daughter's child with a nice Italian man whose life, like her daughter's, had been cut short.

At least, that's what she'd told herself, the thing about blood being thicker than water and all that. But that was before she'd found out her daughter had conceived a child with…with that man.

Bianca got out of her car and glanced up as if she knew her grandmother would be watching. Her raven hair glistened in the sunlight as her gaze found Marietta at her window. Usually this was where her granddaughter smiled and waved and then hurried inside.

Today she stood there staring up, her face expressionless, her manner reserved. After a few moments, she looked toward the front door, brightened, then rushed in that direction.

Marietta knew then that Ester must have opened the door. Bianca loved the housekeeper. Maybe even more than she loved her grandmother.

That thought left a bitter taste in her mouth. She turned away from the window. Out of stubbornness, she thought about staying where she was and letting Bianca come to her.

But after a few minutes had passed, she couldn't stand it any longer and headed downstairs.

She found Ester and Bianca with their heads together, as she often did. The sight instantly annoyed her. But also worried her.

"I thought you would come upstairs," she said, unable to hide her displeasure.

Both women turned toward her but said nothing. Marietta looked from Ester to Bianca and felt her heart drop.

"What's wrong?" she demanded. "Has something happened?"

"I know, Grandmother. *How could you?*"

Chapter Eleven

DJ rode alongside Beau through the snow-covered pines until behind them the house could no longer be seen. The world became a wonderland of snow and evergreen below a sky so blue it hurt to look at it.

She didn't think she'd ever breathed such cold air. It felt good. It helped clear her head.

The cowboy riding beside her seemed to be lost in the beauty of the country around them, as well. What was it about him? She felt drawn to him and his cowboy code of honor. Yet all her instincts told her to be careful. He was the kind of man a woman could fall for, and she would never be the same after.

She'd spent her life never getting attached to anything. This man, this place, this Cardwell family all made her want to plant roots, and that terrified her. For so long she'd believed that was a life she could never have. But maybe, if the doll and photo were her mother's family reaching out to her and not a threat...wasn't it possible that she could finally live a normal life?

They rode up a trail until the trees parted and they got their first good view of Lone Peak across the valley and river. This late morning it was breathtaking. The stark peak gleamed against the deep blue of the big sky. No wonder this area had been named Big Sky.

"It's incredible, isn't it?" Beau said as he stopped to look.

DJ reined in beside him to stare out at the view. The vastness of it made her feel inconsequential. It wasn't a bad feeling. It certainly made her problems seem small.

"Beautiful," she said on a frosty breath.

"Yes, beautiful."

She felt his gaze on her. Turning in the saddle, she looked into his handsome face. He looked so earnest... "Okay, you got me out here. Why?"

"I thought you'd like the view."

She shook her head. "If you're trying to find a way to tell me that you're stepping away from this—"

"I don't break my promises." He pushed back his Stetson and settled those wonderful blue eyes on her. His look was so intense, she felt a shudder in her chest. "We need to talk about what Zinnia told you. But first I've got some bad news. I called your father this morning." She braced herself. "He was attacked at the prison. He's in the hospital."

DJ wasn't sure what she'd been expecting. Not this. The news was a blow. For years she'd told herself that she hated him, that she never wanted to see him. She blamed him for her childhood. She blamed him for keeping her family from her. She bit her lip to keep from crying. "Is he—"

"It sounds serious."

DJ nodded, surprised how much her chest ached with unshed tears. "You think his attack…" She didn't need to finish her sentence. She saw that he thought whatever she had to fear, he suspected it was connected to her father's attack. "Why?"

"I don't know yet. But I will find out."

He sounded so sure of himself that she wanted to believe him capable of anything. Wasn't that why her father had cashed in on the promise? He must have believed that if anyone could keep her safe, it would be Beau Tanner.

"You think I'm in danger?"

"I do. We need to find out what is going on. We need to find your mother's family."

"But nothing's happened. Yes, I was left a doll and photo of people I didn't know at the time…"

"They broke into your house to leave it."

"But what if it's my mother's family trying to let me know about them?"

He shook his head. "DJ, if that was the case, then why wouldn't they have simply picked up the phone or mailed the doll and the photo with a letter?"

"You see the doll and photo as a threat?" Hadn't she at first, too?

"I agree, someone wants you to know. The question is, why? Given what we learned from Zinnia Jameson..."

She saw where he was going with this. "It could explain a lot about my childhood. I always felt as if we were running from something. What if my father was trying to keep my mother's family from finding us? You don't think he might have...kidnapped me, do you?"

STACY WASN'T SURPRISED when Jimmy showed up at her part-time job at Needles and Pins, the shop that her sister's best friend, Hilde, owned. He pushed open the door, stepped in and stopped dead.

He was taking in all the bolts of fabric as if realizing he was completely out of his element. Stacy watched him, amused. James Ryan afraid of coming into a quilt shop. It endeared him to her more than she would have liked.

"Jimmy?" she said as if surprised to see him. Actually she wasn't. After she'd run into him yesterday, it had been clear he was hoping to see her again. That he had tracked her down... Well, it did make her heart beat a little faster. She'd always thought of him as the love of her life.

He came in, moving to the counter where Stacy was cutting fabric for a kit she was putting together. "James."

"Right. Sorry. Old habits... Do you like the colors?" she asked as she finished cutting and folded the half yard neatly. "Tangerine, turquoise, yellow and brown."

"Beautiful," James said without looking at the fabric. "So, this is where you work?"

"Part-time. I help Dana with the kids and work some on the ranch."

"Busy lady," James said. "I just wanted to make sure we were on for tonight."

She felt her heart do that little hop she'd missed for a long time. "Tonight. Right." She hesitated, torn. Then heard herself say, "Sure, why not?" even though a few not so good memories had surfaced since his call last night.

"Good. I can't wait." He sounded hopeful, and the look in his eyes transported her straight back to high school, when he used to look at her like that.

Stacy felt a lump in her throat. Was it possible they were being given a second chance at love? It seemed too good to be true. "I never thought I'd see you again."

He grinned, that way too familiar grin that had made her lose her virginity to him all those years ago. "Neither did I. Life is just full of surprises. Great surprises. So, I'll pick you up on the ranch. Which cabin did you say was yours?"

"The one farthest to the right on the side of the mountain. You remember how to get to the ranch?"

He laughed. "Like it was yesterday."

MARIETTA HAD TO sit down. She moved to a chair and dropped into it. Her heart pounded in her ears and she feared it would give out on her. She'd feared something like this might happen and had told Roger as much.

"Maybe the best thing would be to tell Bianca," she'd said.

"Have you lost your mind? Once you do that, you're basically admitting that this…woman has a right to part of your estate," Roger had said. "No, there is a better way to handle this, and Bianca never has to know."

Why had she listened to that man?

Bianca brushed back her long, dark hair and glared at her grandmother. "What have you done?"

Marietta's gaze shifted to Ester. She'd never seen such determination in the woman's expression before. Her lips were clamped tightly together and her eyes were just as dark and angry as Bianca's.

"What have you *done?"* she wanted to demand of her housekeeper. Yes, Ester was nosy. And yes, she'd been acting odd lately. But Marietta had never dreamed that she would go to Bianca. She'd trusted the woman. A mistake, she saw now.

Bianca crossed her arms over her chest. "Isn't there something you want to tell me, Grandmama?"

Use of that pet name was almost Marietta's undoing. She lived only for Bianca. Everything she'd done was for this precious granddaughter.

"Tell you?" she echoed, stalling for time.

"Tell me the truth," Bianca demanded, raising her voice. "Do I have a sister?"

Marietta had known when her dying daughter had confessed she'd conceived a child with Walter that this day might come.

Now she realized how foolish she'd been to think she could keep something like this a secret. Although her daughter and Walter had certainly managed. It was clear that Ester had known about the other child, probably from the beginning. That realization hurt more than she wanted to admit.

It would be just like Carlotta to have shared this information all those years ago with the woman who'd practically raised her. Suddenly she recalled Ester at the sewing machine in her tiny room. She'd been startled and tried to hide what she was doing. Marietta had thought she was trying to disguise the fact that she wasn't working like she was supposed to be.

But now she remembered what the housekeeper had been working on. Dolls. There'd been two identical dolls! Two rag dolls, and yet Bianca had always had only the one.

Betrayal left a nasty taste in her mouth. Her gaze darted to Ester. "I want you out of my house!"

"No!" her granddaughter cried, stepping in front of the housekeeper as if to shield her. "Do not blame Ester for this. If you fire her, you'll never see me again." The ultimatum only made the betrayal more bitter. "If it wasn't for Ester, I might never have known that I have a sister you've kept from me all these years."

"I wasn't the one who kept it from you all these years. That was your mother—and Ester." She could see now that Ester had been collaborating with Carlotta for years. Had she been stronger, she would have strangled the woman with her bare hands. "It's Ester who has known for so long, not me. Your mother didn't bother to tell me until she was near death. If you want to blame someone—"

"I'm not here to place blame. My mother had her reasons for keeping it from me. I suspect those reasons had something to do with you. But I won't blame you, either." Bianca stepped toward her. "I just want to know about my sister."

"She isn't your *sister*. She's only half—"

Her granddaughter waved a hand through the air. "She's my *blood*."

That it could hurt even worse came as a surprise. "Your *blood*?" she demanded. "Watered down with the likes of a man…" She sputtered. Her contempt for Walter Justice knew no words.

Bianca dropped to her knees before her grandmother and took both of Marietta's hands in hers. "I want to know about her. I want to know all of it. No more secrets. Grandmama, if you have done something to hurt my sister…" She let go of Marietta's hands. The gesture alone was like a stab in her old heart.

"Get me the phone!" she ordered Ester. She called Roger's number. It went directly to voice mail. She left a message. "Fix this or else."

BEAU COULDN'T HELP but laugh. "Kidnapped you?" He shook his head as he and DJ dismounted and walked their horses to the edge of the mountainside to look out at the view. "I think anything's possible. But I got the impression from your father that somehow your mother's family didn't know about you. And now they do."

"And that puts me in danger?"

He turned to gaze into her big, beautiful brown eyes, wanting to take away the pain he saw there. He'd been trying to save this woman in his dreams for years. Now here she was, all grown up, and he still felt helpless.

"DJ." His hand cupped the back of her neck. He drew her closer, not sure what he planned to do. Hold her? Kiss her? Whatever it was, he didn't get the chance.

The sound of the bullet whizzing past just inches from her head made him freeze for an instant, and then he grabbed and threw her to the snowy ground as he tried to tell from which direction the shot had come.

"Stay down! Don't give the shooter a target," he ordered as he drew his weapon from beneath his coat.

Nothing moved in the dark woods behind them. Only silence filled the cold winter air for long moments.

"The shooter?" she repeated, sounding breathless.

In an explosion of wings, a hawk came flying out of the pines, startling him an instant before he heard the roar of a snowmobile.

"Stay here!" he ordered DJ as he swung up into the saddle.

"Wait. Don't..."

But he was already riding after the snowmobiler. He crested a ridge and drew up short. The smell of fuel permeated the air. Below him on the mountain, the snowmobile zoomed through the pines and disappeared over a rise. There was no way he could catch the man. Nor had he gotten a good look at him.

He swore under his breath as he quickly reined his horse around and headed back to where he'd left DJ.

She'd gotten to her feet but was smart enough to keep the horse between her and the mountainside.

"Are you all right?" he asked. He'd been sure the bullet had missed her. But he'd thrown her down to the ground hard enough to knock the air out of her.

Clearly she was shaken. She hadn't wanted to believe she was in any kind of danger. Until now. "Did you see who it was?" she asked.

"No, he got away. But I'll find him or die trying."

ANDREI COULDN'T BELIEVE he'd missed. It was the cowboy's fault. If he hadn't reached for her right at that moment... But he knew he had only himself to blame. He'd been watching the two through his rifle scope, mesmerized by what he saw. They were in love.

He'd found something touching about that. He'd been in love once, so long ago now that he hardly remembered. But as he watched these two through the scope, he'd recognized it and felt an old pang he'd thought long forgotten.

Fool! Andrei was shaking so hard he had trouble starting the snowmobile. He'd never really considered that he might get caught. As long as the coin toss came up heads, he'd known his luck would hold.

Now, though, he feared his luck had run out. He ripped off his glove and tried the key again. The snowmobile engine sputtered. He should have stolen a new one instead of one that had some miles on it.

He tried the key again. The engine turned over. He let out the breath he hadn't even realized he'd been holding and hit the throttle. He could outrun a horse.

As he raced through the trees, he felt as if his whole life was passing before his eyes. All his instincts told him to run, put this one behind him, forget about Dee Anna Justice.

But even as he thought it, he knew it couldn't end this way. It would ruin his luck, ruin everything. He would make this right because his entire future depended on it.

He was almost back where he'd started a few miles from the main house on Cardwell Ranch when he lost control of the snowmobile and crashed into a tree.

Chapter Twelve

DJ couldn't quit trembling. It had happened so fast that at first she'd been calm. She'd gotten up from the ground, staying behind her horse as she watched the woods for Beau. Had someone really taken a shot at them? Not them. *Her*.

She'd never been so relieved to see anyone as Beau came riding out of the pines toward her and dismounted. He'd given chase but must have realized there was no way he could catch the man. She'd heard the snowmobile engine start up, the sound fading off into the mountains.

Still, she didn't feel safe. "You're sure he's gone?" she asked now as she looked toward those dark woods.

"He's gone. We need to get back to the ranch and call the marshal. I can't get any cell phone coverage up here."

Her legs felt like water. "If you hadn't tried to kiss me again…"

He grinned. "Maybe next time… That's right. I

told you there wouldn't be a next time. I'm usually a man of my word."

She could tell he was trying to take her mind off what had just happened. "I guess you have a kiss coming."

"Glad you see it that way." He looked worried, as if what had almost happened hadn't really hit her yet. Did he expect her to fall apart? She was determined not to—especially in front of him.

She could tell he was shaken, as well—and worried. His gaze was on the trees—just as it had been earlier.

"Why would someone try to kill me?" she demanded. This made no sense. Nor could the same person who'd sent her the doll and the photograph be behind it. That had to be from someone in her family who'd wanted her to know about them.

But she remembered her father's fear when he'd seen the photo. Who was he so afraid of?

"All this can't be about something my father did over thirty years ago," she said, and yet it always had something to do with him. She thought about what Zinnia had told them. "Apparently this person really carries a grudge." She could see that Beau wasn't amused.

"We're going to have to find your grandmother."

"Marietta Pisani. You think she's hired someone to shoot me? Why now?"

"I wish I knew. But maybe it's what your father said. They didn't know about you and now they do."

She shook her head. "They don't even know me. Why would they want to kill me?"

He shook his head. "From what Zinnia said, it could involve money."

"If that's true, no wonder my father told me my mother died in childbirth. He was actually trying to spare me. How do you like that?" She let out another bitter laugh as she turned to look at the cowboy. "So now they want me dead."

"If your mother died a few months ago, maybe that was when the rest of the family found out about you. It must have come as a shock."

"My mother chose her family and their money over me."

"I'm sure it wasn't an easy choice."

She hated the tears that burned her eyes. "I am their flesh and blood. Wouldn't they want to meet me before they had me killed?"

He reached for her, drawing her into his strong chest. She buried her face in his winter coat. "Let's not jump to conclusions until we know what's going on, okay?"

She nodded against his chest. "Why didn't my father tell me the truth when I showed him the photo?" she asked, drawing back.

"I'm sure he regrets it. He swears that when you came to him, he didn't know what was going on."

She pulled away. "My father lies."

BEAU STARED AT her slim back as she swung up onto her horse. She was reasonably hurt by what she'd learned from Zinnia, but she was trying so hard not to show it. "I don't think he's lying about this."

"Someone else knew about me." She turned to look at him. "That person sent me the doll and the photo."

He hated to tell her that maybe the doll and the photo might merely have been a way of verifying that she was indeed Walter Justice's daughter. When she'd received the items, she headed straight for the prison—and her father, whom she hadn't acknowledged in years.

"But now they're afraid I'll go after the money." She shook her head. "After years of believing I had no family other than my father, now I have so much that some of them have put a price on my head. I don't know what to say."

Beau didn't, either. "You could contact them, possibly make a deal—"

"I don't want their money!" She spurred her horse.

He had to swing up into the saddle and go after her. The woman could handle a horse. He rode after her, sensing that she needed this release. Her horse kicked up a cloud of snow that hung in the air as he caught up and raced like the wind alongside her.

Her cheeks were flushed and there was a steely glint in her eyes that told him of a new determination.

"You'll help me find out who is behind this?" she asked as they reined in at the barn.

"You know I will. But first we have to report this." Swinging down from the saddle, he called the marshal's office. Hud told them to stay there. Good to his word, he was there before the horses were unsaddled and put away in the pasture.

Hud sent several deputies up into the woods to the spot Beau told him about. They'd be able to find it easily enough by following the tracks.

Once inside, he steered them both into the kitchen. "Here," Hud said, shoving a glass of water into DJ's trembling hands. "I have something stronger if that would help."

She shook her head and raised the glass to her lips, surprised she was still trembling. She'd believed she could take care of herself. Now she was just thankful that Beau had been there. What if it had been she and Dana who'd ridden up into the mountains?

"I'll take that something stronger," Beau said to Hud, and he poured him a little whiskey in a glass. Beau downed it in one gulp but declined more.

"This doesn't make any sense," DJ heard herself saying. "It had to have been an accident." She wanted the men to agree with her. But neither did. She could tell that Beau was convinced this was what her father had feared.

She listened while Beau told Hud in detail what he knew. Then she said, "If I brought whatever this is—"

"We'll get to the bottom of this," Hud said. "I'll tell you what Dana would. You're with family. We aren't going to let anything happen to you."

But even as he said it, DJ could see that he was worried. The last Dee Anna Justice had come here and brought trouble. The real Dee Anna promised herself that wouldn't be the case this time. She had hoped she'd find the answers she needed in Montana. Now she worried that she was endangering the family she'd just found.

She would leave as soon as she could get a flight out.

But even as she thought it, she had a feeling she wouldn't be leaving alone—if Beau had anything to do with it.

ANDREI GRIMACED IN pain as he finished bandaging his leg in his motel room. The snowmobile accident was just another bad sign, he told himself. And yet he had survived it with minimal damage.

He'd managed to push the wrecked snowmobile off into a gully where it wouldn't be found—along with some of the debris that had been knocked off it when he'd hit the tree. He'd gotten away. That alone should have been cause for celebration, since it was the closest he'd come to being caught.

Had he not missed, the cowboy would have been trying to save his beloved instead of racing on horseback in an attempt to catch her would-be killer.

He stood now to test his leg and, groaning in pain, sat back down. He wouldn't be climbing any more power poles, that was for sure. But he wasn't going to let this mishap change anything. He'd be fine by tomorrow, he assured himself.

The problem was that now DJ and her protective cowboy would know he was out here. They would be even more careful than they had been at first. He would have to wait—and watch. In good time, he told himself. And he still had time. He could complete this before his birthday, and he would.

He checked his phone. There were two messages from the man who'd hired him. Andrei didn't bother to listen to them. Whatever the man wanted, it didn't matter. This had become personal. Nothing could stop him now.

MARSHAL HUD SAVAGE leaned back in his chair in his den on the ranch to look at Beau. Dana, Stacy and the kids had returned. Not wanting to upset them, he'd suggested the two of them talk in his den. They'd known each other for years—just not well. Their cases had never overlapped until now.

"So, Dee Anna's father hired you?" Hud asked.

Beau liked to keep things simple. He'd learned that years ago when dealing with his father—and the law. He nodded. "He asked me to watch over his daughter."

"He wasn't more specific than that?"

"No."

"And how exactly did he know about you?"

"I guess he could have looked in the phone book under private investigators," he said, dodging the truth.

Hud nodded. "Seems odd, though, asking you to keep an eye on her while she's here where her cousin's husband is the marshal."

"Not really." He softened his words with a wry smile. "Walter Justice is in prison. It could be he doesn't trust law enforcement."

The marshal chuckled at that. "Point well-taken, given what we know about Walter." He studied Beau openly for a moment. "You had taken DJ for a horseback ride."

"To talk. DJ's trying to find out more about her family."

"Dana said the three of you went to visit Walter's high school girlfriend, Zinnia Jameson?"

Beau nodded. "DJ knows nothing about her father's past. We were hoping Zinnia could provide some answers."

"That's what you had to talk to DJ about?"

He could tell that Hud was suspicious, since it had been Beau who'd taken her to a spot where a shooter had almost killed her.

"We needed to talk about what we'd learned, but also, I had to give her some bad news. Her father was shanked in prison."

"I'm sorry to hear that. I get the impression from Dana that DJ and her father aren't close."

"No, but he's still her father."

Hud sighed. "There's something about your story… Tell me again what the two of you were doing right before you heard the shot and felt the bullet whiz past."

Beau laughed. He had great respect for the marshal. The man had sensed he hadn't told him everything. "I was about to kiss her. I'd pulled her closer…"

The marshal nodded smiling. "You were trying to kiss her?"

He grinned. "Unfortunately the shooter took a potshot at us before that could happen."

"So, this is more than a job for you?"

Beau didn't want to get into the whole story of the first time he saw DJ and how he'd never forgotten her. "There's been some attraction from the start."

"I can understand that. It's those Justice women." He turned serious again. "You didn't get a good look at him?"

"No. Nor the snowmobile. Earlier I thought I heard one in the distance, but I didn't think anything about it. It's December. Everybody and his brother have one of the damned things, and the mountains around here are riddled with old logging roads."

"But you're convinced the bullet was for DJ?"

"Depends on how well the man shoots. If he was aiming for me, he can't hit the side of a barn. But if he was aiming for DJ, he's good. Really good. If I hadn't drawn her toward me when I did…"

"You're thinking a professional?"

"I am."

"You have any idea why someone would want Dee Anna Justice dead?"

Beau hesitated. He understood why Hud had wanted to talk to him alone. DJ was Dana's family. Hud would have done anything for his wife.

"It might have something to do with her mother's family," Beau said after a moment. "I'm going to shadow her until we find out what's going on. I don't have much to go on." He told the marshal the names of both mother and grandmother.

Hud wrote them down. Marietta and Carlotta Pisani. "Why would her own flesh and blood want to harm her?"

Beau shook his head, thinking of Cain and Abel. He couldn't help but wonder about DJ's half sister. "There might be money involved."

"Grandmama, you're scaring me. Tell me what you've done," Bianca demanded as her grandmother hung up the phone. "I'm assuming that was Roger you called. He hired someone to find my sister and then what?" She shook her head as if too disappointed in her grandmother to talk for a moment.

Ester had dropped into a chair across from them.

Marietta looked at her precious granddaughter.

Her heart was in her throat. What if the man Roger had hired had already accomplished what he'd paid him to do? Now she realized that she could lose the one person who mattered to her.

"Do you have any idea how much I love you, how much I have tried to protect you—"

Bianca's look stopped her cold. "What have you done?"

"It might not be too late."

"Too late for what?"

Marietta waved that off and tried to rope in her thoughts. Roger would already have called if it was done. Of course he'd stopped it. Roger was too smart to go against her wishes on this. She reminded herself he was so smart that apparently he'd been stealing from her for years. She was the matriarch of this family, but Roger was a man she'd leaned on since her husband had died all those years ago.

"Listen to me. I'm trying to make this right." Her fear of losing Bianca's love, though, was a knife lodged in her chest.

"Tell me everything you know about her," Bianca said, sitting down next to her.

There was no keeping it from her now. "I don't know very much, just what your mother told me. Her name is Dee Anna Justice."

"So after Mother told you, did you try to reach her? You just said it might be too late."

So Ester *hadn't* told her everything. Marietta

thought she still might stand a chance of regaining Bianca's love, her trust. "You have to understand. Your mother was very young. She fell in love with this man from Montana who was all wrong for her. Fortunately she realized her mistake…" She almost said, *"before it was too late,"* but that had been what she'd thought at the time.

Now she knew that it *had* been too late. Carlotta had given birth to Walter Justice's child—and kept the truth from nearly everyone.

On her deathbed, Carlotta had cried, saying it was Marietta's fault that she'd had to keep Dee Anna a secret all these years.

"I wanted my child with me. I needed my child with me. But you had made it clear that if I didn't come home, forget about Walter and go to Italy to stay with my aunt…"

"You are going to blame me for this?" she'd demanded.

"I had to give up my child because of you."

No, Marietta had argued. "You gave up your child for *money*. You knew I would cut off your allowance if you stayed with that man. It was your choice."

Had her daughter thought that one day she could just come home with the child and all would be forgiven? Or had she given up on that foolish idea when she'd met the nice Italian man she'd married and become pregnant with *his* child?

"Surely Walter Justice would have gladly given up the child had you demanded it," she had pointed out to her daughter.

"You're wrong. He loved me. He loved Dee Anna. He would never have let you get near her, knowing how you felt about him. But, Mother, now you can make up for the past. Now you have a chance to know your *first* granddaughter."

Carlotta must have seen her expression, because her own hardened. "Or not. Whatever happens, it's on your head now, Mother."

MARIETTA REALIZED BIANCA had asked her a question.

"Why did you hate my sister's father so much?" Bianca asked again, accusation in her tone.

"He was a crook. All he was interested in was our money."

"*Money.* Why does it always come back to that with you?"

"He's serving time in prison. I think that tells you what kind of man he is." She hated that her voice rose, that she sounded like a woman who'd lost control of her life. A woman who was no longer sure of the stand she'd taken. A woman who would die drowning in regret.

Bianca rose. "I want to meet my sister."

"Stop calling her that!" Marietta snapped irritably. "She is merely your mother's mistake."

Her granddaughter looked horrified at her words.

She regretted them instantly. "You don't understand," she pleaded. "This woman isn't one of us. If she is anything like her father, she'll demand part of your inheritance. I know you think you don't care about the money, about the family legacy—"

"It is the family *curse*," Bianca said. "That's what mother called it. She used to wish her family was dirt-poor."

Marietta wanted to laugh. Her extravagant daughter would not have liked being poor, let alone dirt-poor.

Bianca's eyes narrowed. "So this is about money. You're afraid she will want money."

"No, I was willing to give her money. It's about you, Bianca. I don't want you to be hurt. Contacting this woman can only—"

"Tell me how I can find her," Bianca said, cutting her off.

She swallowed and looked to Ester. "Why don't you ask *her*?" she said, pointing to her housekeeper. "She seems to be well-informed."

Ester's gaze met hers, unspoken secrets between them. The housekeeper hadn't told Bianca about the hit man. But she'd hinted at it. Did Marietta really want her to tell everything she knew?

"I'm asking *you*," her granddaughter said.

Marietta sighed. She knew when she'd lost. Wasn't it possible that Dee Anna Justice could already be dead? If so, Bianca would never forgive her. And the family legacy could already be gone, thanks to Roger. She had only herself to blame for all of this. But to lose both Bianca and her fortune would be unendurable.

"She's at the Cardwell Ranch near Big Sky, Montana, but—"

"I'm going to find her," Bianca said with more determination than Marietta had ever seen in her.

As she started to leave, Ester said, "I'd like to go with you."

Bianca shot a look at her grandmother and seemed to hesitate. "Can you manage alone with your bad heart?"

"I've been on my own before," Marietta snapped, wondering how she *would* manage. "Don't worry about me."

"I'll call when I find her," Bianca said.

Everything she cared about was walking out that door. She didn't think her heart could break further. She was wrong, she realized as she saw Ester's suitcase by the door and knew that she might not see either of them again.

"WE HAVE TO find out who's behind this," Beau told DJ before they left Cardwell Ranch. "I thought we'd go by my office in Bozeman. I should warn you about my assistant. She's... Well, you'll see soon enough."

He wasn't surprised when Marge did one of her

eyebrow lifts as they walked in. What did surprise him was how quickly she took to DJ.

Like a mother hen, she scurried around, getting coffee, offering to run down to the cupcake shop for treats.

"We're fine. We won't be here long," he told her with an amused and slightly irritated shake of his head. He ushered DJ into the office, saying, "I'll be right back," and closed the door behind her.

Turning to Marge, he said, "What is going on with you?"

"Me?" She gave him her innocent look.

"This isn't a *date*. DJ is a *client*, of sorts. This one is…off the record, but it is still work. Nothing more."

"DJ, huh?"

He shook his head. "Why do you take so much interest in my love life?"

"*What* love life?" she said, fiddling with some papers on her desk.

Beau ignored that jab. "Are you hoping to get me married off?"

"I never said a word."

"You don't have to." He started for his office, but something was bothering him. Turning back to her, he said, "I have to know. DJ walks in and you instantly like her. You've never liked any of the women I've dated, and you've never done more than share a few words with them on the phone. What is different about this one?" he demanded, trying to keep his voice down.

Marge smiled. "You'll remember this one's name."

Chapter Thirteen

DJ pulled up a chair next to Beau as he turned on the computer and began his search. She felt surprisingly nervous sitting this close to him. It brought back the memory of being in his arms, of his mouth on hers. There was something so masculine about him.

"You all right?" he asked as she moved her chair back a little. "Can you see okay?"

She nodded and tried to breathe. "How long has Marge been with you?"

"Since I started. She's like a mother hen." He shook his head. "But I couldn't run this office without her." She heard true admiration and caring in his voice. She also sensed a strong loyalty in him. Look how he'd agreed to protect her based on a promise he'd made so many years ago.

"I like her."

He glanced over at her. "And she likes you. Believe me, it's a first." Their gazes locked for a moment. She could feel the heat of his look and remembered how he'd almost kissed her up on the mountain.

At the sound of his assistant on the other side of the door, he turned quickly back to the computer. "Okay, let's see what we can find out about your grandmother. Marietta Pisani. There can't be that many, right?"

DJ thought about how this had started with the doll and the photo. Her father's letters had led them to Zinnia, who'd told her more about her father— and mother—than she'd ever known. Leave it to her father to tell Beau that the doll and photo might have something to do with her mother's family. Why couldn't he have told her that?

Because he'd been lying to her since birth, she reminded herself. She felt a stab of guilt. He was in the hospital, badly injured. She'd called but hadn't been able to learn much—just that he was in stable but serious condition. She told herself he was tough. He'd pull through. She hoped it was true.

"Your father told you that your mother was dead, but that your grandmother Marietta is still alive, right?" Beau was saying. "Marietta Pisani. Is there any chance she's related to the noble Pisani family of Malta? Descendants of Giovanni Pisani, the patrician of Venice?"

"I have no idea," DJ said.

"Maybe you'll get a chance to ask her," he said and motioned to the screen. "I found only one in the right age group. A Marietta Pisani of Palm Desert, California."

DJ swallowed the lump in her throat. This was the woman who'd had her daughter's marriage to Walter Justice annulled. "What do we do now? You can't think that my grandmother..." Her words faltered. She could see from his expression that he could think exactly that.

Her father had also thought it. Why else would he have asked Beau to protect her? But surely she didn't need protecting from her own grandmother?

"We call her," Beau said and reached for the phone.

It took Marietta a while to calm down after Bianca and Ester left. At first she was just scared. Scared that she'd lost everything. Then she was furious with Ester for butting into her family business. She'd tried to reach Roger but suspected he was not picking up. The coward.

At some point, she'd have to find out if there was any money left. But right now, it was her least concern. Her daughter would have thought that funny, she realized. The joke was on her, she realized. Roger had stolen her money. All that worry about the family legacy and now she realized that if she lost Bianca, nothing mattered.

When a middle-aged woman arrived with a suitcase in hand claiming to be Ester's younger sister, May, she almost turned her away.

"I'm not like Ester. I'll see to you, but don't think you can browbeat me the way you do her."

Marietta was offended. "I don't browbeat anyone."

May huffed and slipped past her. "Just tell me where my room is. Then I'll see about getting you fed. I cook whatever I can find to cook and you eat it. That's the deal."

With that, the woman had sashayed off in the direction Marietta had pointed.

This was what her life had come to? She almost wished that she'd died this morning before she'd seen that little red sports car drive up.

But then she wouldn't have seen her precious granddaughter. Not that their visit had gone well.

She tried Roger's number again. Again it went to voice mail. It was in God's hands, she told herself. God's and Bianca's and Ester's and whomever Roger had hired.

She prayed that Dee Anna Justice was still alive. She just didn't want Bianca hurt. But who knew what this Dee Anna Justice was like? She couldn't bear the thought of Dee Anna rejecting Bianca. If there was any money left, she knew her granddaughter would gladly share it with her…sister.

Marietta made the call. She had to take control of her life again, one step at a time, until her old heart gave out.

As STACY DRESSED for her date, she felt torn between excitement and worry. Did she really believe that she and James could start over again after all these years? Maybe she was hanging on to a first-love fantasy James, one who had never existed.

"What has he done for a living since high school?" Dana had asked. She didn't know. "What does he do now?"

"I think he said real estate."

Her sister got that look Stacy knew only too well.

"You remember him," Stacy said. "You liked him in high school, didn't you?"

"I didn't know him," Dana said. "But I do remember that he broke your heart."

"It wasn't his fault. He thought his ex-girlfriend was pregnant..." She stopped when she saw Dana's expression. "He did the right thing by her. He married her."

"I suppose so," her sister said. "Just...be careful. It's not only you now. You have to think of Ella."

She'd thought only of Ella since her daughter's birth. There hadn't been any men, not even one date. But now she could admit that she felt ready. She wanted a husband and a father for Ella and said as much to Dana.

"There is nothing wrong with that," her sister said, giving her a hug. "Maybe James is that man. Maybe he's not. Give it time. Don't let him rush you into anything."

She knew what Dana was getting at. James had rushed her into sex in high school. She hadn't been ready, but she'd feared that she would lose him if she didn't give in to him.

As she finished dressing, Stacy told herself she wasn't that young, naive girl anymore. If James thought she was, then he was in for a surprise.

ROGER SWORE WHEN he saw how many times Marietta had called. He didn't even bother to check the voice mails. He knew she'd be demanding to know what was going on. He'd called the man who'd hired the hit man and had finally heard back.

"He rushed the job and missed," the man told him. "Now he has to fix it. So back off. These things take time. Worse, now she knows someone is trying to kill her. Also, the marshal is involved."

Roger felt sick to his stomach. "You told me that he would make it look like a shooting accident. This isn't what my boss wanted at all. Call him off."

"I'll do what I can. He isn't answering his phone."

Could this get any worse?

"He's going to want the rest of the money. You'd best have it ready for him," the man warned.

"Of course." Roger hung up, sweating. His phone rang again. He saw that this time it was the accountant he'd been working with. Marietta. She was checking the trust funds. He was dead meat, he thought as he let her call go to voice mail.

He decided he'd better listen to Marietta's message. What he heard turned his blood to ice.

"Bianca knows! She and Ester are headed for Cardwell Ranch in Montana. If anything happens to them, I'll have you killed in prison, and you know I can do it. I might not have as much money as I once did, but I still have power."

He disconnected, not doubting it for a moment. He looked around the room. He couldn't wait any longer. She knew that he'd been embezzling money for years from the family trust funds. He'd hoped that he could win it back, but his gambling debts were eating him alive. If the thugs he owed didn't kill him, then Marietta would.

His cell phone rang again almost instantly. He put it on mute, telling himself he would throw it in the ocean the first chance he got and buy a new one. Then he stepped to the suitcase. His passport and the plane tickets were on the table by the door. He picked them up, took one last look at the house he had mortgaged to the hilt and, suitcase in hand, walked out.

MARIETTA LET OUT a scream of pain when she heard an estimate of how much money was missing from the trust funds.

May rushed into the room. "If you're not bleeding, this had better be a heart attack or a killer snake in the room."

"I want to die."

May shook her head. "Let me get a knife."

"I've made a horrible mess of things."

"Haven't we all? If you don't want your supper burned, die quietly while I get back to the kitchen."

Marietta could hear her heart pounding and welcomed death. What had she done? Her mind wouldn't stop racing. All she could think about were the mistakes she'd made. She had another granddaughter. Bianca would have loved having a sister. She used to ask for one all the time. It broke Marietta's heart.

The irony was that Carlotta's second husband hadn't been much of a step up from Walter. Gianni had some shady dealings before his death. But at least he'd come from a good Italian family with money.

She had wanted so much for her daughter.

And yet Carlotta still hadn't married well.

"Playing God wearing you out?" May asked as she brought in her dinner tray.

"Do you always say whatever you think without regard to whether or not it is proper?" Marietta demanded.

May smiled. "Not much different from you, huh?"

"I'm not hungry," she said, trying to push the tray away.

"Too bad. I'm going to sit right here until you eat. Ester said all I had to do was keep you alive. I figure you're too mean to die, but just in case..." May pushed the tray back at her and sat down, crossing her arms.

Marietta glared at her for a moment before picking up her fork. If she had to eat to get the woman out of her room, she would.

"You know nothing about any of this," she said. May chuckled.

"If I thought Ester was talking behind my back—"

"What would you have done? Fired her?" May shook her head. "Ester didn't have to tell me anything about you. I saw it in the sadness in her eyes. She's been loyal to you, just as our mother was. You don't realize how lucky you are that she put up with you all these years. Anyone else would have put a pillow over your face years ago."

"I feel so much better knowing you'll be staying with me until Ester comes back," she said sarcastically.

"You think Ester is coming back?"

Marietta stopped, the fork halfway to her mouth. She didn't want to acknowledge her fear that Ester was gone for good. "She won't leave me alone. Not after all these years."

"Because of your sweet disposition? Or because you pay her so much?"

She felt her face heat but said nothing as she concentrated on her food again. This was what her life had come to, she told herself. She was an old woman alone with an ingrate who had nothing but contempt for her. She half hoped the woman had poisoned her food.

Chapter Fourteen

The phone rang. Marietta snatched it up, hoping it was Bianca calling. Maybe she'd changed her mind about going to Montana, about meeting her half sister, about…everything.

"Hello?"

"Is this Marietta Pisani?"

"Yes." Her heart pounded.

"My name is Beau Tanner. I'm a private investigator in Montana. I'm calling about your granddaughter."

"Bianca?" Montana? Was it possible Bianca and Ester had gotten a flight out so soon and were now in Montana?

"No, Dee Anna Justice."

She gripped the phone so hard that it made her hand ache. She held her breath. Hadn't he said he was a private investigator? Shouldn't it be the police calling if Dee Anna Justice was dead?

"What about her?" she asked, her voice breaking.

"You recognize the name?"

"Yes. She's my granddaughter. What is this about?"

"I was hoping you would tell her," the private eye said. "I'm putting her on the phone."

"Hello?"

Marietta heard the voice of her first granddaughter and felt the rest of her world drop away.

"Hello?" the voice said again.

Marietta began to cry uncontrollably.

May came in, saw what was happening and took the phone. "I'm sorry. She can't talk right now." She hung up the phone. Turning, she demanded, "Where do you think you're going?"

Marietta had shoved away the food tray, gotten to her feet and gone to her closet. Pulling out her empty suitcase, she laid it on the bed and began to throw random clothing into it. "I'm flying to Montana."

May took in the suitcase the older woman had tossed on the bed. "Do you really think that's a good idea given your…condition? Let alone the fact that you might be arrested when you land."

So Ester had shared information with her sister. Marietta knew she shouldn't have been surprised. "You've been in on all this?"

May smiled. "It was my son who left the doll and a photo of her mother, grandmother and Carlotta's second husband for DJ." She sounded proud of what she'd done. "Ester was afraid of how far you would go. She said DJ couldn't be brought off. She wouldn't have wanted a cent of your money. So all of this was a huge waste on your part."

Marietta finished throwing a few items in, slammed her suitcase and zipped it closed. She'd been surrounded by traitors. "You couldn't possibly understand why I've done what I have."

"Why you used money to keep your daughter away from a child that she loved?" May demanded. "Did Carlotta tell you how she cried herself to sleep over that baby you forced her to give up?"

"Forced her? It was her choice. Just like it was her choice to marry the man. So easy to blame me, isn't it?"

May put one hand on her bony hip. "What would your daughter think now if she knew that you were trying to kill that child?"

Marietta swallowed. She wanted to argue that it was all Roger's doing. But she'd trusted him to handle it. Her mistake. All she'd thought about was erasing the existence of Dee Anna Justice to save the family.

"Help me with my suitcase."

May didn't move.

"I'm going to save the woman. Does that make you happy?" she barked.

"*The woman?* She's your grandchild. She's your blood. She's Bianca's sister."

"I don't have time to argue with you." She shook

her head. "None of you know this Dee Anna Justice. What if she wants nothing to do with our family? What if she rejects Bianca? What then?"

"Bianca is a strong woman. She will survive. I think you might underestimate the connection they have," May said. "Ester kept in touch over the years with Dee Anna's father. She saw the girl grow up."

"My suitcase."

May stepped forward, slid the suitcase from the bed and began to wheel it toward the front door. "You best hope that you're not too late."

It was already too late in so many ways.

"Some woman took the phone and said she couldn't talk. Before that it sounded like she was…crying," DJ said as she saw Beau's anxious expression.

He took the office phone and replaced it in its cradle. "At least now we know that she's the right one."

"I guess. She was definitely upset. But upset to hear from me or to hear that I'm still alive?" She could see he was even more convinced that her grandmother was behind what had happened earlier today on the mountain.

"What now?" As if she had to ask. "The would-be assassin will try again, won't he?" She didn't give him time to answer. "I can't stay at Cardwell Ranch," she said as she pushed to her feet. "I can't endanger my cousin and her family—"

"That's why I want you to move in with me."

She blinked. "No, I couldn't."

"If it makes you feel any better, I have a...friend staying with me. Leah."

"I see." A friend, huh? Was that what he called it? She realized how little she knew about this man.

"I can protect you better on my home ground."

"I think everyone would be better off if I just left Montana."

"You're wrong. But if you leave, I'm going with you. Sorry, but you're stuck with me until this is over."

She stared at him even though she'd expected this. "You can't be serious, and for how long?"

"As long as it takes. But if you could just give me a few days and not leave, it would be better. If whoever shot at you is still here, it will give me the chance to catch him."

She didn't like the sound of this. She'd come to care about this man. She didn't want to see him get killed protecting her and said as much.

"Have more faith in me," he said with a grin. "Let's go get your things." They drove in silence to the Cardwell Ranch.

Dana put up a fight when Beau told her his plan.

"Christmas is only a few days away," she argued. "DJ is family. She should be here with us."

"With luck, this will be over by Christmas," he told her. "Hud thinks it is best, too."

"Hud." With that one word, Dana looked resigned.

DJ hugged her. "I'm so sorry. I would never have come here if I thought it might be dangerous for your family."

"You have nothing to be sorry for," Dana said. "You take care of her," she said to Beau. "I'm depending on you."

"I hate this," DJ said as he drove them off the ranch. "I hate that I involved them and, worse, you. You're only doing this because of some stupid promise you made when you were a boy to a man who had no right to ask anything of you."

Beau was quiet for a long moment as he drove. It almost surprised her when he finally spoke. "The first time we met, I wished that I could help you," he said without looking at her. "I've regretted it ever since."

She spoke around the lump that had formed in her throat. "I don't want you to get killed because of me."

"I don't want that, either," he said with a chuckle. "But I'm not that ten-year-old anymore." He finally glanced over at her. "I can help you. I know what I'm doing."

She looked away, fighting back tears. All this was because of her father falling in love with the wrong woman? Now he was in the hospital possibly dying and she was… She was in Montana with a cowboy who was determined to save her.

They hadn't gone far when Beau turned off the highway and crossed a narrow bridge that spanned the Gallatin River before driving back into the canyon. At the heart of the valley was a large log house. Behind it was a red barn and some outbuildings. A half-dozen paint horses raced around in a large pasture nearby.

"This is where you live?" she asked, a little awed by the beauty of the scene.

"Do you like?" he asked and glanced over at her.

"I love it." She felt a lump form in her throat. She could see Beau here. "You're a real cowboy."

He laughed. "You're just now realizing that?"

She turned to look at him. She was just now realizing a lot of things, she thought as she stared at his handsome profile in the last light of the day.

Jimmy was late picking her up, making Stacy have even more second thoughts. But he seemed so glad to see her that she pushed them aside and tried to have a nice time.

He took her to one of the local restaurants, ordered them both a cocktail and drained half his glass before letting out a sigh. He actually looked nervous, which made her laugh and forget her own nervousness.

"So tell me about this cousin staying on the ranch," he said.

"Dee Anna Justice. She's the daughter of my mother's brother, whom we didn't know anything about." She really didn't want to talk about DJ, though. "So, what did you say you're doing in Big Sky again?"

"Working. A brother no one had ever heard of?"

"Working at what?" she asked, wondering why he was so interested in the Justice side of the family.

"This and that." He drained his glass. The waiter came over and before Stacy could look at her menu, James ordered for both of them, including more drinks. "You don't mind, do you?" he asked after the waiter had already left.

She shook her head, although she did mind. "How long did you say you've been back?"

"Did I say? A few weeks. Actually, I'm looking for a job. Anything opening up on Cardwell Ranch?"

She couldn't help but laugh. "What do you know about working on a ranch? As I recall, you hated helping on your uncle's."

"I forgot what a good memory you have." That didn't sound like a compliment. The waiter came with their drinks and he downed his quickly.

"Jimmy—"

"But you can't seem to remember that I go by James now." He was clearly irritated and not trying to hide it.

"Sorry. Why did you ask me to dinner tonight?"

He leaned back, giving her a what-do-you-think look. "I thought for old times' sake…" He shrugged. "You dating someone?"

Fortunately their meals came. They talked little.

Jimmy ate as if he hadn't had a meal in days. He devoured his steak and then asked her if she was going to finish hers. She'd lost her appetite early on in the date, so she gladly slid her plate over and let him clean it.

What had she been thinking? Her sister was right. The Jimmy Ryan she'd been in love with all those years ago wasn't the man sitting across from her.

"Ready?" he asked as he signaled the waiter for his bill.

Turning, she spotted Burt Olsen, their mailman. He nodded and smiled at her. He appeared to be picking up something to go.

Stacy just wanted this date to be over. When Jimmy saw her looking at Burt, he threw an arm around her waist and propelled her toward the door.

"Maybe I should drive," she said as they started toward his truck.

"I don't think you should think." He still had hold of her as they neared the pickup. He opened the driver's-side door and practically shoved her in, pushing her over to get behind the wheel.

"Jimmy—James."

"I remember you being a lot more fun," he said, gritting his teeth.

And vice versa, but she said nothing as she saw Burt getting into his vehicle. He'd been watching the two of them. And she knew that if she said anything to Jimmy, it would turn into a fight. Burt was the last person she wanted seeing her and Jimmy fighting. She told herself that Jimmy hadn't had that much to drink—and it was only a short drive to the ranch.

Neither of them spoke during the drive. As they crossed the bridge, he glanced over at her. "You hear me?"

She hadn't realized he'd said anything. "I'm sorry?"

"I'm sure you are." He drove on into the ranch and pulled up in front of her cabin. "So which one is this cousin of yours staying in?"

She pointed to the last one at the other end of the row. She knew what was coming, but Jimmy was out of luck if he thought she was going to invite him in.

"Thanks for dinner," she said as he shut off the engine. She reached for her door handle. But before she could get it open, he leaned over and grabbed her hand to stop her.

"I'm sorry about tonight. It wasn't you. I got some bad news right before I picked you up. I should have canceled." He drew back his hand.

"What kind of bad news?" she asked out of politeness.

"An investment. It fell through. I was counting on it."

She hoped he didn't ask her for money. "I'm sure you'll be able to get a job."

"A *job*." He said the last word like it tasted nasty

in his mouth. "Just not on your ranch, huh? You don't even know what I do for a living."

"A little of this and that is all you told me." She reached for the door handle again.

This time his hand came around the back of her neck. He clamped down hard enough to take her breath away. "You're kind of a smart mouth. I do remember that about you."

Stacy tried to wriggle out of his grasp. "Stop!" she said as he pulled her toward him as if to kiss her. "I said *stop*!" That feeling of déjà vu hit her hard. This was what had happened in high school, only then she'd thought that he was so crazy about her he just couldn't help himself. She knew better now.

Chapter Fifteen

Leah looked up expectantly as Beau entered the kitchen. She smiled quickly as if covering her disappointment. Who had she expected? Her husband? Or someone else?

Her gaze went to DJ, her expression one of surprise and something else. Jealousy?

"This is DJ. She's going to be staying with us. DJ, Leah."

"No last names?" Leah asked, pretending to be amused.

He walked to the stove. "You cooked?"

"Don't sound so surprised. I'm a woman of many talents."

Beau could believe that somehow, even though he hadn't been around Leah in years. She'd always seemed…capable.

"Looks like you made enough for three," he said, lifting the lid on one of the pots and glancing into the oven, where what looked like a Mexican casserole bubbled. Looking up, he said, "You must have been expecting company."

She shook her head, but not before he'd seen that moment of hesitation. Her laugh wasn't quite authentic, either. But he wasn't about to get into it with her now.

He turned to DJ. "Let me show you to a room."

"It was nice meeting you," Leah called after them.

"You, too," DJ said over her shoulder, and then added only for his ears as they climbed the stairs and rounded a corner, "She doesn't want me here. Wouldn't it be better if I—"

"She isn't my *girlfriend*. She's the wife of my former best friend. I have no idea what she's doing here, so what she wants is really of no interest to me."

DJ WAS SURPRISED at his words. He'd been so protective of her, and yet he seemed angry at the woman they'd left downstairs.

He saw her surprise as they reached the end of the hall, and he started to open a door but stopped. "I don't mean to seem cold, but it's what she's not telling me about her and her husband that has me worried."

"It's none of my business."

He studied her openly. "Come on, let's hear it. I can tell there is something on your mind."

"Did the two of you ever—"

"No. She was always Charlie's girl, and before you ask, no, I was never interested in her."

"It's odd, then, because she seems very possessive of you."

He shrugged and pushed open the door to a beautiful room done in pastels.

"What a pretty room."

He didn't seem to hear her. "I'm right next door if you need me. Leah is downstairs in the guest room."

"Who's room is this?" She realized her mistake at once. "I shouldn't have asked."

"I was engaged to a woman with a young daughter. This was going to be her room, but it didn't work out."

"I'm sorry."

He shook his head. "Looking back, I loved the thought of having a child more than I loved having her mother as my wife." He took a step toward the door. "Get unpacked if you like, then come downstairs. Let's find out if Leah really can cook or not."

After he left, DJ looked around the beautiful room. He'd made it so pretty for the little girl. There was such love in the room. She felt sad for him. How lucky that child would have been in so many ways.

She took her time unpacking what little she'd brought, giving Beau time with Leah. Whatever was going on between them, she didn't want to be in the middle of it. She had enough troubles of her own.

Taking out her phone, she put in a call to the

prison. Her father was still in serious condition at the hospital.

She withdrew the photo of her mother from her purse and sat down in the white wooden rocker to study it. This woman had been her mother. She hadn't died in childbirth. No, instead, she'd apparently given up her first child to make her family happy, then married another man and had another child.

But what, if anything, did this have to do with the man who'd shot at her? According to what Beau had been able to find out, her mother really had died recently. So who wanted her dead? The grandmother who'd refused to talk to her? Zinnia had said that her mother's family had money. Surely it couldn't be that simple.

But her father had known the moment he looked at the photo. Her mother's family had found her, and that had terrified him enough that he'd pressured Beau Tanner to protect her.

But what about the other daughter? The one who'd had the doll? What about her half sister?

As Jimmy grabbed at her, Stacy swung her fist and caught him under the left eye. He let out a curse. His grip loosened and she shoved open the door, only to have him drag her back. He thrust his hand down the front of the dress she'd bought for the date. She heard the fabric tear as he groped for her breasts.

With his free hand, he grabbed her flailing wrists and dragged her hard against him. "You like it rough? You'll get it rough," he said, squeezing her right breast until she cried out.

Stacy hardly heard the driver's-side door open. Jimmy had been leaning against it and almost fell out as the door was jerked open.

"She said stop," a familiar male voice said.

Jimmy let go of her, pulling his hand from inside her dress to turn angrily toward the open door—and the intruder. All he got out was "What the he—" when a fist hit him between the eyes.

Stacy saw it only out of the corner of her eye. The moment Jimmy let go of her, she slid across the seat and climbed out of the pickup. That was when she saw who her savior was. Mailman Burt Olsen's face was set, his voice dangerously calm. "You go on inside now, Ms. Cardwell. I'll take care of this."

She hesitated only a moment before scurrying up the steps. Once on the porch, she turned back. Just as she'd feared, Jimmy was out of the truck and looking for a fight. He took a swing, but Burt easily ducked it and caught Jimmy in the jaw with a left hook. He toppled back toward the open truck door. Burt doubled him over as he fell, shoved him back into the truck and closed the door.

"He won't be bothering you anymore tonight," the mailman called over to her. "But if you need me to stay…"

She almost couldn't find the words, she was so surprised. "No, I'm fine now. But thank you, Burt."

He tipped his baseball cap. Past him, she could see where he'd parked his car and walked up the mountainside. He'd come to her rescue after seeing what had been going on at the restaurant, and all she could think was that he'd let his supper get cold to do it.

Inside the cabin, she locked her door just in case Jimmy—*excuse me*—James, didn't get the hint. The man was a fool, but he wasn't stupid, she told herself. Glancing out the window, she saw that Burt was waiting for Jimmy to leave. She was relieved when a few minutes later she heard his truck start up and drive away.

In the bedroom, she saw that her dress was ruined. She tossed it into the trash. Thinking about Burt Olsen, she had to smile. She'd never seen this side of him before.

JIMMY HAD NEVER been so furious. Who the devil had that man been? Stacy's sweetheart? Nice of her to mention, if that was the case. But he'd called her Ms. Cardwell. Must have been a hired man.

Not that it mattered. He'd sat for a moment, stunned and bleeding and planning his revenge. The lights went out in Stacy's cabin. He considered breaking down the door but realized he wasn't up to it. There was always another day. The woman would pay.

As he started the truck's engine to drive out of the ranch, he thought about the dude who'd hit him. If he ever saw him again…

He hadn't gone far when his headlights flashed over someone in the shadows of one of the outbuildings. For a moment he thought it was the man who'd attacked him. He slowed and saw his mistake. This man, who ducked behind the barn, was much larger, dressed in all black. He was carrying something. The moonlight had caught on the barrel of a rifle.

Jimmy sped on by, pretending not to have noticed. As he drove down the road to where it dropped over a rise, he realized he'd seen the man before. It was the lineman he'd seen on one of the power poles when he'd driven in earlier.

"Lineman, my ass," he said to himself as he quickly pulled over and cut the engine. He pulled his hunting knife from under the seat.

It was time to take care of the competition. He quietly opened his door and stepped out into the winter night. He could see his breath as he started back toward the barn. The pro must be waiting for DJ Justice to return. Stacy had said earlier that she thought DJ had left with some neighboring cowboy.

Well, Jimmy had a surprise for the man, he thought with a grin. He'd take care of the pro, and then maybe he'd double back for Stacy. He was feeling much better suddenly. And if the bitch thought she would get rid of him that easily, she was sadly mistaken.

BEAU FOUND LEAH setting the table for three. "So, what's going on?"

She looked up as if she'd been lost in thought and he'd startled her. "Supper is almost ready. I made a casserole. I'm not much of a cook, but—"

"I'm not talking about food. What are you really cooking up?"

Leah gave him a blank look. "I told you—"

"You were expecting a package, but…" She started to interrupt. He stopped her with an angry slash of his hand through the air. "What are you really doing here? Earlier you told me that you and Charlie were in trouble and you needed my help."

"I was wrong. This is something that will have to work itself out on its own. I can't involve you."

"You've already involved me. I'm tired of whatever game this is that you're playing. Tell me what the hell is going on."

She slowly put down the plate she'd been holding, straightened the napkin and silverware and then finally looked up at him. "There is a lot I can't tell you. Charlie and I…we've become involved in some… covert work. Our latest…assignment didn't go so well. I got out. Charlie…" Her voice broke. "We made a pact years ago that if we ever got separated, we would meet here." Her eyes glistened. "Because you were always our one harbor even in college."

"Why didn't you tell me that right away?" he asked quietly as he considered what she'd told him.

"Because I didn't come here to involve you in anything. You and your friend aren't in any danger. Charlie's and my work is done far from here. No one knows I'm here except Charlie. I made sure that I wasn't followed."

He had a million questions, which he suspected she wasn't going to answer anyway, but the creak of the stairs told him that their conversation was over. At least for now.

He'd never been a trusting man—thanks to his father. He hated the way his mind worked. He questioned what most people told him. Leah was at the top of the list right now.

The knock at the door made them both jump. Beau had taken off his shoulder holster and hung it by the door. He stepped to it now and motioned for Leah to go into the den. DJ had stopped on the stairs. One look at him and she'd frozen in midstep.

Another knock, this one harder. Beau strode to the door and pulled his weapon. Stepping to the side, he opened the door, the weapon ready.

He felt a moment of shock when he looked at the rugged, clearly exhausted man standing there. *"Charlie?"*

Chapter Sixteen

Andrei heard the car engine as someone left the ranch. He frowned as he waited for the sound of the vehicle crossing the bridge and didn't hear it. He listened. A chill moved up his spine. He had been watching the house from his hiding spot. But now he stopped at the edge of the barn and sniffed the air.

The vehicle had definitely not crossed the bridge. Nor had it turned back. He would have heard it. That meant that it had stopped. The winter night was so quiet he could hear the ice crack on the edge of the river. He heard the soft click of a car door being closed and readied himself.

The driver had seen him. That rattled him enough. But the driver was also trying to sneak up on him. That meant the person would be armed with some kind of weapon.

All Andrei had was a rifle. But he didn't want to shoot and call attention to himself. So he would wait until the man reached the corner of the barn and then he would jump him. He was ready.

He pressed his back against the side of the barn at the corner and waited. This would complicate things, he thought, on a job that was already complicated as it was. But since his accident, he'd been frustrated. Maybe this was exactly what he needed to let out some of that anxiety.

It had always been more satisfying to kill someone with his bare hands than shoot them from a distance. Given that his leg still hurt like hell, he probably should have walked away. But it was too late now. A twig under the snow snapped close by. No time to make a run for it even if he could have run. This could end only one way. One of them was about to die.

The man came around the corner of the barn. The large knife blade in his hand caught the winter light.

"I'M AFRAID WE won't be joining you for dinner," Charlie said after he and Beau had hugged like the old friends they were. His gaze met his wife's. She stood a few feet away, tears in her eyes and relief etched on her face. She hadn't moved since Beau had opened the door, as if to give the two men some time.

"We need to get going, but it is great seeing you," Charlie said.

"That's it?" Beau demanded as Leah scurried down the hall to the guest room, returning moments later with her overnight bag. She stepped to her husband's side and pressed her face into his neck for a moment, his arm coming around her. The hug was hard and filled with emotion. Clearly this was the package she'd been waiting for.

Charlie had always been good-looking. Now, even though he appeared a little haggard, his smile was infectious. "It is so good to see you. One of these days, we'll be back permanently. I hope we can get together then, have a couple of beers and talk. But right now…"

Beau shook his head. He'd been angry at Leah for not telling him what was really going on. But he couldn't be angry with Charlie, his old friend. "Just be careful." He shook Charlie's hand and watched as the two disappeared down the road. Beau saw car lights flash on and heard the sound of an engine, and then they were gone as if they'd never been there.

He turned to look at DJ.

"Are you all right?" she asked.

He gave her a quick nod. "I hope you're hungry. We have a lot of casserole to eat."

She moved toward the kitchen. "I'd better take the casserole out of the oven, then."

"Maybe we could just sit in front of the fire and have a drink while it cools down a little. I could use one." He moved into the living room and stepped to the bar.

"Wine for me," she said when he offered her a

bourbon like the one he'd poured for himself. "You don't have to say anything."

He ran a hand over his face and let out a bitter laugh as they sat in front of the fire. "I didn't trust her. Leah was one of my best friends years ago, and when she showed up…" He met DJ's gaze. "I hate how suspicious I am of people. I question everything."

DJ WAS SILENT for a moment before she said, "Your father was a con man, right?" He nodded, making her smile. "And you expect us to be trusting?" She laughed at that. "We grew up with no stability, no security, no feeling that everything was going to be all right. How did you expect us to turn out?"

"You might be the only person who understands. But you seem to have it all together."

"I *do*?" She laughed again. "It's just an act." The wood popped and sparked in the fireplace. Golden warm light flickered over them. She took a drink of her wine and felt heat rush through her.

"You think we will ever be like other people?" he asked.

"Probably not. But maybe at some point we won't have so much to fear."

"I remember the first time I saw you. Those big brown eyes of yours really got to me. I wanted to save you. I told myself that if I ever got the chance, I would do anything to help you."

She met his gaze and felt a start at what she saw

in those blue eyes. Thinking of how it had felt to be in his arms, she yearned for him to hold her. It wouldn't change anything. There was still someone out there who wanted to kill her, but for a while...

Except she knew that just being held wasn't enough. He made her feel things she'd never felt with another man. She would want his mouth on hers, his body—

"We should probably eat some of that casserole," she said, getting to her feet. She no longer wanted temporary relief from her life. Could no longer afford it. Tomorrow morning would be too hard on her. Too hard to let go of this cowboy and the connection between them that had started so many years ago.

Beau seemed to stir himself as if his thoughts had taken the same path as her own. "Yes."

They ate in a tense silence, the fire crackling in the living room, the kitchen warm.

"This is good," she said, even though she hardly tasted the casserole. She was glad when the meal was over and wished that Beau hadn't insisted on helping her with the dishes.

"I think I'll turn in," she said as soon as they'd finished cleaning up the kitchen.

He looked almost disappointed. "See you in the morning."

She watched him go to the bar and pour himself another bourbon. When she headed up the stairs, he was standing in front of the fireplace, looking into the flames.

Her steps halted, but only for a moment. She *did* understand him. They had a bond that went back all those years. She felt as if she'd always known him. Always…felt something for him.

That thought sent her on up the stairs to her room. But she knew she wouldn't be able to sleep. She felt lost, and she knew that Beau did, too.

She lay in bed, remembering the older woman's voice on the phone. Her grandmother. And hearing the woman crying so hard that she couldn't talk. Was this really a woman who wanted her dead?

BEAU HAD JUST put the coffee on the next morning when he heard DJ coming down the stairs. The phone rang. He'd had a hell of a time getting to sleep knowing that DJ was only yards down the hall. He couldn't help worrying about what the day would bring. A phone call this early in the morning couldn't bode well.

"Beau Tanner," he said.

"It's Marshal Savage, Beau. I've got some news. A man by the name of Jimmy Ryan, a suspected small-time hit man, was found dead on the ranch this morning. Based on the evidence we found in his vehicle, we believe he was the shooter yesterday. He had a high-powered rifle and a photo of DJ with a target drawn on her face."

"You said he's dead?"

"His throat was cut. Earlier last evening, he'd gotten into an altercation with a local man here on the ranch. We suspect the disagreement ended on the road on the way out of the ranch. Jimmy Ryan was found some yards off the road by one of our barns."

He couldn't believe what he was hearing. "So, it's over?" he said and glanced at DJ.

"It certainly appears that way."

"Do we know who hired him?"

"Not yet. We'll continue investigating. I'll let you know if anything new turns up. Dana wanted to make sure that DJ knew. She has her heart set on her cousin staying until after Christmas, and since it is so close…"

"I'll tell DJ and do everything I can to keep her in Montana until after Christmas." He ended the call and found himself grinning in relief. It seemed impossible. The hit man had gotten into an argument with someone and it ended in his death? He wouldn't have believed it if it wasn't for what the marshal had found in the man's vehicle.

"That was the marshal," he said. "They think they have your hit man."

"They caught him?"

Beau didn't want to get into the details this early in the morning, so he merely nodded. "He's dead, but they found evidence in his vehicle that makes it pretty apparent that he was the shooter. I don't know any more than that."

"I heard you ask if they knew who'd hired him."

He shook his head. "I'm sure they'll check his cell phone and bank account. But all that takes time. Hud did say that Dana would be heartbroken if you didn't stay for Christmas. He begged me to get you to stay." He held up his hand as he saw that she was about to argue. "Whatever you decide, I'm sure you don't want to leave until we know more. So…while we're waiting, I have an idea. Have you ever cut your own Christmas tree?"

She looked surprised before she laughed. "I've never even had a real tree."

He waved his arms toward his undecorated living room with Christmas so close. "Never bothered with it myself. But this year, I feel like getting a tree. You up for it?"

DJ HAD A dozen questions, but she could see that they would have to wait. To her surprise, she was more than up for getting a Christmas tree. "After that amazing news, I'd love to go cut a tree."

"Great. Let's get you some warm clothes, and then we are heading into the woods."

She loved his excitement and her own. Clearly they were both relieved. The man who'd shot at her was dead. It was over. She had planned on being gone by Christmas. She still thought that was best. But what would it hurt to help Beau get a Christmas tree?

Dressed as if she was headed for the North Pole, DJ followed Beau through the snow and up into the pine trees thick behind his house. They stopped at one point to look back. She was surprised again at how quaint his place looked in its small valley surrounded by mountains.

"You live in paradise," she said, captured by the moment.

"It is, isn't it?" He seemed to be studying his house as if he hadn't thought of it that way before. "Sometimes I forget how far I've come." He glanced over at her. "How about you?"

She nodded. "We aren't our parents."

He laughed. "Thank goodness." His gaze lit on her.

DJ saw the change in his expression the moment before he dropped the ax, reached out with his gloved hand and, cupping her neck, drew her to him. "I believe you owe me a kiss."

His lips were cold at first and so were hers. The kiss was short and sweet. Their breaths came out in puffs as he drew back.

"You call that a kiss?" she taunted.

His gaze locked with hers. His grin was slow, heat in his look. And then his arms were around her. This kiss was heat and light. It crackled like the fire had last night. She felt a warmth rush through her as he deepened the kiss. She melted against him, wrapped in his arms, the cold day sparkling around them.

When he pulled back this time, his blue eyes shone in the snowy light in the pines. Desire burned like a blowtorch in those eyes. He sounded as breathless as she felt. "If we're going to get a tree…" His voice broke with emotion.

"Yes," she agreed. "A tree." She spotted one. It was hidden behind a much larger tree, its limbs misshapen in its attempt to fight for even a little sunlight in the shadow.

"Dana has this tradition of giving a sad-looking tree the honor of being a Christmas tree." She walked over to the small, nearly hidden tree. "I like this one. It's…"

He laughed. "Ugly?"

"No, it's beautiful because it's had a hard life. It's struggled to survive against all odds and would keep doing that without much hope. But it has a chance to be something special." There were tears in her eyes. "It's like us."

He shook his head as if in wonder as he looked at her, then at the tree.

"Okay, you want this one? We'll give the tree its moment to shine."

"Thank you." She hugged herself as she watched him cut the misshapen pine tree out of the shadow it had been living under.

He studied the tree for a moment before he sheathed his ax. "Come on, tree. Let's take you home."

BIANCA DIDN'T ASK until they were both on the plane and headed for Montana. "You knew about her? My sister? Since the beginning?"

Ester nodded. "Your mother couldn't keep anything from me."

"But you didn't tell Grandmama?"

The housekeeper sighed. "Your mother made me promise, and what good would it have done? I'd hoped that in time... Marietta sent your mother to Italy to stay with an aunt there while she quietly had the marriage annulled. The next time I saw your mother, she was married and pregnant with you."

Bianca shook her head. "How could she have just forgotten about the baby she left behind?"

"She never forgot. When I made that rag doll for you, your mother insisted I make one for your... sister."

"That's why you left my doll and a photograph in her apartment."

"I had a nephew of mine do it. I wanted to tell her everything, but I was afraid."

She turned to look at the older woman. "Afraid my grandmother would find out."

"Afraid it would hurt you. I'd done it on impulse when I realized your grandmother was trying to find DJ."

"DJ? Is that what she calls herself?"

"It was a nickname her father gave her."

"So you saw her occasionally?"

Ester sighed. "Only from afar. Her father insisted. I would tell your mother how she looked, what she was wearing…" Tears filled her eyes. "It was heartbreaking."

"She was well cared for?"

"Well enough, I guess. Her father wouldn't take the money offered him by your grandmother's lawyer at the time the marriage was annulled."

Bianca scoffed. "So maybe he isn't as bad a man as Grandmama makes him out to be."

"Your grandmother had good reason given that he never amounted to anything and is now in prison. But he raised your sister alone and without any help from the family. I admire him for that, even though it was not an…ordinary childhood for DJ. I know he feared that the family would try to take her. I was the only one he let see her—even from a distance."

"I always wanted a sister," Bianca said more to herself than to Ester.

"I know. And I always felt sad when you said that growing up, knowing you *had* a sister. But it wasn't my place to tell you."

"Until now. Why *did* you tell me now?" Bianca asked, turning in her seat to face Ester.

Ester hesitated. Bianca could tell that the housekeeper didn't want to say anything negative about her grandmother.

"Because you were afraid of what my grandmother might do," Bianca said, reading the answer on the woman's face.

"No, I was afraid of what Roger Douglas would do. I knew I couldn't stop him, but you could."

"But did I stop him in time?" Bianca looked out the plane window. *She had a sister.* Her heart beat faster at the thought. How could her grandmother have kept something like this from her? Worse, her own mother?

She'd seen how her grandmother had used money to control Carlotta. She had always told herself that she wouldn't let Marietta do the same thing to her and yet she had taken all the gifts, the Ivy League education, the trips, all of it knowing that she'd better bring the right man home when the time came.

"Do you think she'll be all right by herself?" she asked Ester.

The housekeeper smiled. "Your grandmother is much stronger than any of us give her credit for. But I called my sister while you were getting our tickets. She can handle Marietta."

"Thank you. No matter what she's done, she's my grandmama."

"She is that."

Bianca closed her eyes. She'd lost her father at an early age, so all she'd had was her mother, grandmother and, of course, Ester. It was Ester who had kissed her forehead each night, who got her off to school, who doctored the scrapes and lovingly applied the medicine. Her mother had always seemed lost in thought. She assumed that no one noticed how much wine she had at night before she stumbled to her room in the huge house overlooking the ocean.

Now Bianca wondered if giving up her first child had haunted her. When she'd often had that faraway, sad look in her eyes, was it Dee Anna Justice she was thinking about?

If so, she knew she should have been jealous of the hours her mother had been off—if even in her mind—with her other daughter. Had she loved her more? It didn't matter. She felt no jealousy.

Opening her eyes, she looked out the plane window again. They were almost there. She wasn't going to let anything—or anyone—keep her from her sister.

Bianca had always felt as if there was something missing from a life in which she seemed to get anything she wanted.

What she'd really wanted, though, was a sibling. She remembered asking her mother once if she could have more children. She'd wanted a brother or sister so badly.

"Don't be ridiculous," her mother had snapped.

"I know Daddy's dead, but can't you find another man—"

"Stop it, Bianca. Just stop it." She'd sent her to

ask Ester about dinner. As Bianca had left the room, she'd looked back to see her mother go to the bar to pour herself a large glass of wine. Her mother had been crying.

She'd never seen her mother cry before, so she'd made a point of keeping her desire for a sibling to herself after that.

Now she understood those tears. Had her mother ached for that other daughter just as Bianca had ached for her?

The captain announced that they would be landing in the Gallatin Valley soon.

"Maybe we should call this ranch," Ester said, but Bianca shook her head.

"I don't want them to know we're coming." When Ester seemed surprised by that, she added, "If you were my sister, would you want to meet us? I can't take the chance she might leave to avoid us, especially if Grandmama has...done something."

Ester nodded.

Bianca reached over and took the housekeeper's hands. "I hope she likes me."

Ester's eyes filled with tears. "She will love you."

STACY WAS IN SHOCK. When she'd told her sister what had happened last night, she hadn't heard yet about Jimmy. "Burt wouldn't kill Jimmy. He wouldn't kill *anyone*."

"You said yourself that you'd never seen him so

angry and that he hit Jimmy twice," Dana argued after she had told Stacy about Jimmy's body being found out by the barn, his throat slit. "Anyway, Hud has only taken Burt in for questioning based on what you told me."

Stacy got up from the kitchen table to pace. She'd lived around her brother-in-law long enough to know how these things worked. Hud would have to go by the evidence. "Burt hit him. Jimmy fought back. Of course there will be some of Burt's DNA on him, but that doesn't mean Burt killed him."

She couldn't believe this was happening. Jimmy was dead. But that wasn't as upsetting as Burt being blamed for it.

"Hud will sort it all out." Her sister eyed her with a mixture of pity and concern. "I thought you weren't interested in Burt."

Stacy hated to admit that she'd felt that way until last night. But she'd seen a different side to him. "He rescued me from Jimmy. He followed us from the restaurant because he was worried about me. And with good reason. I don't know why I agreed to go out with Jimmy. I made excuses for him back in high school when he forcibly took my virginity. He said he was so turned on by me that he couldn't stop himself and it was my fault."

Dana shook her head in obvious disgust. "All while you were saying no?"

She nodded. "I tried to push him off…but I didn't

try hard enough back in high school. Last night I would have fought him to my dying breath."

Her sister didn't look pleased to hear that. "I told Hud what you told me, but he will want your side of the story," Dana said, picking up the phone.

Stacy shook her head as her sister started to hand her the phone. She realized that Hud would have questioned her earlier, but she had taken the kids to school. "I'm going down to his office. He's questioning the wrong person."

"I should warn you, he'll want to know where you were last night," her sister said behind her.

She turned slowly. "You can't think *I* killed Jimmy."

"Of course not."

"If I was going to kill him, I would have done it years ago after he raped me. I think until last night, I was still blaming myself for what happened—just as he let me do all these years. Now that I think about it, if Burt hadn't shown up when he did…" She looked up at her sister. "I would have killed him before I let him rape me again."

She went out the door, knowing that she'd made herself look guilty. Better her than Burt.

Chapter Seventeen

Andrei heard the news at breakfast in a small café at Meadow Village. He had tried to go about his day as usual, pretending to be one of the many tourists at the resort for the holidays. No one paid him any mind, since he wasn't limping as badly as he had been.

It wasn't like he could go to Cardwell Ranch. The law was crawling all over the place. Dee Anna Justice wasn't there, anyway. He hadn't seen her or the cowboy since the two had driven away together. But he was convinced she would be back, and the ranch was much easier for his purposes than driving back into the narrow canyon to get to the private investigator/cowboy's house. He assumed the cowboy would take her to his place.

As he ate, he knew that after last night this would be the perfect time for him to just leave, put all of this behind him.

But his pride wasn't going to let that happen.

"The man's throat was cut," a woman whispered to another at the next table. She shuddered and then leaned closer to the other woman. "I heard from my friend at the marshal's office that the dead man was a professional killer."

That caught his interest. His heart began to pound, making it hard to hear what else the woman was saying. So, there had been another contract. He swore under his breath. Things were getting so damned complicated.

"Do they know who did it?" the other woman whispered back.

"Well...you know Burt Olsen?"

"The *mailman*?"

Out of the corner of his eye, he saw her nod. "I heard he's been taken in for questioning. He had gotten into a fight with the man earlier that night."

"Burt Olsen? I just find that hard to believe. That he would...cut a man's throat." She shivered. "Burt always seems so nice."

"You know what they say about deep water."

Poor Burt, he thought. Common sense told him that he'd been given the perfect way out. The cops would think they had their man. Dee Anna Justice would let her guard down. So would her cowboy. He could still finish this job, collect his money and leave the country before his birthday. That's how he had to play this while his luck held.

BEAU STOOD UP the Christmas tree in the living room and stepped back to consider it. "Wow, it looks better than I thought it would. Pushed against the wall like that, it really isn't bad." He turned to see DJ smiling at the tree.

"It's beautiful. It doesn't even need ornaments."

He laughed. "That's good, because I don't own any. I thought we could string some popcorn. I'll pick up some lights when I go to town."

His gaze met hers. That kiss earlier had almost had him making love to her in the snow up on the mountain. He stepped to her now. She moved into his arms as naturally as a sunrise. He held her close, breathing in the fresh-air scent of her.

"DJ," he breathed against her hair.

She pulled back to look up at him. What he saw in her eyes sent a trail of heat racing through his veins. She stood on tiptoes to kiss him. Her lips brushed against his. Her gaze held his as the tip of her tongue touched his lower lip.

He felt a shudder of desire. Taking her hand, he led her over to the fireplace. "Are you sure about this?"

"I've never been more sure of anything in my life."

Golden light flickered over them as they began to undress each other. He could feel her trembling as he brushed his lips across hers.

He trailed kisses from the corner of her mouth down to her round breasts. He found her nipple and teased the hard tip with his tongue, then his teeth.

She arched against him as they slowly slid down to the rug in front of the fire. The flames rose. The fire crackled and sighed.

On the rug, the two made love as if neither of them ever had before.

BIANCA AND ESTER landed at Gallatin Field outside Bozeman and rode the shuttle to the car rental agency. While they waited, Bianca looked out at the snow-covered mountains. She'd never driven on snow and ice before. For a moment she questioned her impulsiveness at jumping on a plane and coming here.

Wasn't her grandmother always telling her to slow down, to think things out before she acted? Just the thought of her grandmother made her more determined to get to Cardwell Ranch—and her sister.

"Here's your key," said the man behind the desk. "Your car is right out there. Do you know where you're going?" he asked, holding up a map.

"Big Sky," she said and watched as he drew arrows on the map and handed it to her.

"Maybe we should call," Ester said as they left. "Just showing up at their door… Maybe we should warn them not only that we're coming but that maybe your grandmother did something she regrets."

Bianca shook her head. "I'd rather take my chances. Anyway, call and say what? We have no idea what is going on. For all we know…" Her voice broke. "I know she did wrong, but I still can't get her into trouble. I keep telling myself that Grandmama wouldn't... hurt her own grandchild."

"In Marietta's eyes, *you* are her only grandchild."

"I'm furious with her, but I can't throw her under the bus," Bianca said, making Ester smile.

"I've wanted to do just that for years, but I understand what you're saying. You don't want her going to prison. I don't, either. It's why I called you and told you what was going on."

"We are only about forty miles away." Bianca shot her a look as she drove, following the man's directions from the rental agency. "Roger was the one who hired someone. Maybe she didn't stop him, but it wasn't her idea, right?"

Ester looked away. "I doubt the law would see it that way. She saw Walter Justice as a problem." She shrugged. "Now she sees his daughter as one."

"But Walter is still alive."

"Last I heard, but he's also in prison."

Bianca shot her a look. "You can't think she had anything to do with that!"

Ester shrugged. "I wouldn't put anything past your grandmother. Let's just hope that phone call she made was...real and that she has stopped all this foolishness."

Bianca stared at the highway into the canyon and the steep mountains on each side. "Look what she did to my mother. Forcing her to keep Dee Anna a secret from me. I'm not sure if I can forgive her if something has happened to my sister."

DJ FELT AS if her life couldn't get any better. It was a strange feeling. After years of holding back, of being afraid really to live, she'd given herself to Beau Tanner completely. Her heart felt so full she thought it might burst.

"It is really over?" she asked him the next morning on the way to Cardwell Ranch. Dana had called and invited them over for brunch, saying the crime scene tape was gone and the ranch was back to normal.

Beau squeezed her hand. "You're safe."

Safe. She realized she'd never felt it before. It was a wonderful feeling, she thought as she looked out on the winter landscape. It had snowed again last night, huge flakes that drifted down in the ranch light outside Beau's home. She'd felt as if she was in a snow globe, one with a cozy little house inside. Wrapped in Beau's arms under the down comforter, she'd found paradise.

Last night she hadn't thought about the future, only the present. But this morning as they neared the turnoff to Cardwell Ranch, she couldn't help but think about her mother's family. What now? If it was true that they'd tried to kill her, fearing she wanted their money… The thought made her heart ache.

Beau reached over and took her hand. "It's going to be all right."

She couldn't help but smile at him. Nor could she help but believe him. With Beau in her corner, she felt she could take on the world.

BIANCA TURNED OFF the highway at Big Sky and stopped a few yards from the Cardwell Ranch sign that hung over the entrance. She glanced at Ester, who quickly took her hand and squeezed it.

"You can do this," Ester said. "She's your sister."

She nodded, smiling in spite of her fear, and drove under the sign and across the bridge spanning the river. She felt as if she'd been waiting for this her whole life. Even with all the lost years, she and DJ still had time to get to know each other. If her sister wanted to.

Bianca felt a stab of fear. What if her grandmother was right and this young woman wanted nothing to do with her family? With her?

A large new barn appeared ahead along with a half-dozen cabins set back in the woods. But it was the rambling old farmhouse that she drove to, with the black Suburban parked in front. She saw a curtain move.

"Tell me I'm not making a mistake," she said to Ester.

"Letting your sister know she's not alone in this can't be a mistake," the older woman said.

Bianca smiled over at her. "I don't know what I

would have done without you all these years." She opened her door, Ester following suit.

The steps seemed to go on forever, and then they were on the porch. Bianca was about to knock when the door opened, startling her.

A dark-haired woman in her thirties looked surprised. Was this DJ? Was this her sister?

"I'm Bianca," she said at the same time the woman said, "I'm sorry, I thought you were...someone else."

The woman looked from Bianca to Ester and back. "Did you say Bianca?"

She nodded. "I'm looking for Dee Anna Justice," Bianca said.

"She's not here right now," the woman said excitedly. "But I'm her cousin Dana."

Feeling a surge of relief at the woman's apparent welcome, she said, "I'm her...sister, Bianca."

Dana smiled. "Yes, her sister. What a surprise."

"I hope not too much of a surprise," she said. "This is Ester, a...a friend of mine. Is my sister here?"

"Please, come in," Dana said and ushered them into the warm living room. "I'll call DJ...Dee Anna, and let her know you're here. Please, have a seat. I was expecting her when you drove up."

Bianca sat in a chair by the fire, glancing around at the Western decor. Until this moment, she hadn't felt like she was in Montana. As Ester took a place on the couch next to her, she spotted the Christmas tree.

Dana turned her back, her cell phone at her ear,

and said, "You should come home now," before disconnecting and dialing another number.

When she turned back to them, she saw what they were looking at—and no doubt the expressions on their surprised faces. "That's my orphan Christmas tree," Dana said with a laugh. "It's a long story." She seemed to be waiting for the call to go through, then said, "You aren't going to believe who is sitting in my living room. Your sister! Oh, it's her all right. She looks enough like you that there is no mistake. Okay, I'll tell her." Dana disconnected, smiling. "She's on her way and should be here any minute."

Bianca had never felt so nervous. Ester reached over and patted her hand. "It's going to be fine," the housekeeper whispered.

She nodded, smiling and fighting tears as she heard a vehicle pull up out front. Dana said, "In fact, she's here now."

"ARE YOU SURE you heard right?" Beau asked as he pulled up in front of the house.

Earlier DJ had been sitting cross-legged on the floor in front of the fire, stringing popcorn for their Christmas tree. She had been wearing one of his shirts over a pair of jeans. Her face had been flushed, either from the fire or their lovemaking earlier. She'd looked relaxed, content, maybe even happy. He'd lost another piece of his heart at the sight of her.

Now she looked as if she might jump out of her

skin. "My sister. That must be her rental car. Why would she be at the ranch?" she asked, turning to meet his gaze.

"Apparently she wants to see you."

She shook her head, relieved after her call earlier to the hospital that her father was going to make it. "This is crazy. One minute all I have is my father, and now I have cousins and a *sister*?"

"Who might have hired a hit man to take you out." He pulled out his cell phone. "I'm calling Hud."

"No," she said, reaching for her door. "I want to meet her. I don't need the law there. She isn't going to try to kill me."

He hesitated and finally pocketed the phone. "She'll have to go through me first."

"Seriously, I don't think she'd be here now if she was behind this."

"Apparently you haven't dealt with as many criminals as I have."

DJ laughed and leaned over to give him a kiss. "I have a good feeling about this."

He wished he did.

Chapter Eighteen

DJ couldn't believe that she was going to meet her half sister after only recently finding out that she even existed. "How long do you think she's known about me?" she asked Beau as they walked to the porch steps.

He glanced over at her. "I have no idea."

"Sorry, I just have so many questions."

"Ideally she will be able to answer them all for you. Including who hired someone to kill you."

She looked over at him as they reached the door. "I haven't forgotten. But she's here. That makes her look innocent, don't you think?"

"I'd go with less guilty. But you have no idea what this woman wants. Or why she's shown up now. You have to admit, it's suspicious."

"Which is exactly why I don't think she's involved."

She could tell he didn't agree. "Well, you'll be here to protect me," she said as she reached for the doorknob.

"Yes, I will."

But before she could grab the doorknob, the door swung open, and there was Dana, practically jumping up and down in her excitement.

"Easy," he said behind her. "Let's not get carried away until we find out what is going on."

"I'm glad Beau's with you," Dana said as DJ entered the house. "Hud's on his way," she whispered to Beau loud enough that DJ heard it.

"Really, the two of you..." She stepped into the living room and stopped dead. The woman who rose from the chair by the fire looked more like their mother than even DJ did. DJ stared at her half sister. They looked so much alike it was eerie.

"Bianca?" she asked, although there was little doubt this was the half sister she'd been told about.

"Dee Anna. Or is it DJ? Oh, I'm just so glad you're all right," Bianca said, rushing to her to give her a quick hug. "I have wanted a sister my whole life. I can't believe we were kept apart." She stepped back to take in DJ. "We look so much alike. We could be twins." She let out a nervous laugh.

Out of the corner of her eye, DJ had seen Beau start to move. But he stopped short when Bianca merely threw her arms around DJ.

"I am so glad to see you," Bianca said as she stared at DJ. "I was so worried."

"Worried?" Beau asked only feet away.

Her sister hesitated. An older woman, whom DJ

had barely noticed, stood then and moved to her. There was kindness in the woman's eyes. "I'm Ester."

"Ester," DJ repeated as Bianca stepped back to let Ester take DJ's hand.

"I made your doll," Ester said. "Your father kept me informed on how you were doing over the years. I wish I could have done more."

Tears welled in DJ's eyes. "Thank you. I named her—"

"Trixie. That's why I sent you Bianca's, so you would know there were two of them. Two of you. I couldn't let you go on believing you had no family or that no one cared other than your father."

DJ looked to her sister. "And my grandmother?"

Both women hesitated. Bianca looked guilty, which sent a sliver of worry burrowing under her skin.

"Grandmama is not well," Bianca said.

Ester let out a snort.

Just then, Marshal Hud Savage arrived. "What's going on?" he asked after Dana introduced him as her husband.

"That's just what I was about to ask," Beau said. "Where does a hit man fit into this happy reunion?"

Roger Douglas's cell phone vibrated in his pocket. It surprised him. All the way to the airport it had been buzzing constantly, but it had finally stopped until now. He'd thought, as he'd waited for his flight, that both Marietta and the accountant had given up.

Now he pulled it out, curious which one had decided to give it one more try. He saw who was calling and hurried to a quieter area before answering.

"You didn't tell me about the private investigator who isn't letting her out of his sight," Andrei Ivankov said.

Roger wasn't sure what to say. He'd taken the call only because he'd thought the hit man had finished the job. "I take it you haven't—"

"You take it right."

"It's just as well. The client wants to call off the—"

"I'm sorry, I must have misunderstood you."

"She doesn't want you to finish the job." Roger knew the man was born in Russia or some such place, but his English was better than Roger's own.

"I have been out here freezing my ass off and now she wants me to forget it? I had my doubts about dealing with you. I get paid no matter what, plus extra for my inconvenience, and if I don't get paid, I will track you down and make you wish you'd never—"

"Don't threaten me. There is nothing you can do to me. I really don't give a damn if you kill her or not." He'd raised his voice, and several people had turned to look in his direction. He disconnected the call, then tossed the phone to the floor and stomped it to death. Now a lot of people were staring at him.

Roger felt heat rise up his neck. He'd always prided himself on never losing his temper. But he wasn't that man anymore, he reminded himself. He wasn't the meek lawyer who had to kiss Marietta Pisani's feet.

He'd picked up what he could of the cell phone, tossed it in the trash and started back to his seat when he heard his flight called. Clutching the bag full of Marietta's money, he smiled as he got in line.

It wasn't until he was sitting down in first class, drinking a vodka tonic and dreaming of his new life, the bag shoved under the seat in front of him, that he relaxed. Just a few more minutes.

Glancing out the window, he felt his heart drop like a stone. Two security guards were headed for the plane along with several police officers. He downed his drink, figuring it was the last one he'd get for a while.

"It was a misunderstanding," Bianca assured the marshal. They had all gathered in the dining room around the large old oak table. She turned to her sister. She couldn't believe how much they looked alike. They really could have been twins. "You have to forgive Grandmama. It was her attorney, Roger Douglas. When she found out what he'd done…she was beside herself and demanded he put a stop to it."

Hud and Beau exchanged a glance. "I called the power company. They didn't have any men in our area."

"So the man who was seen on the power pole?" Beau asked.

Hud nodded. "It must have been the shooter."

"Shooter?" Bianca asked.

Dana filled them in on what had happened, first someone taking a shot at DJ, then a man found dead near one of the old barns. "He apparently had been hired to kill DJ."

Bianca's eyes welled with tears. "I'm so sorry. I had no idea. My grandmother had no idea. I'm just so thankful that he missed and that he is no longer a problem."

Hud's cell phone rang. He stepped away to take the call. The room went silent. Bianca prayed that it wouldn't be bad news. She was worried about her grandmother and what would happen now.

"That was the police in San Diego," Hud said as he came back to the table. "They've arrested Roger Douglas. Apparently he made a deal and told them everything, including that he had hired a hit man through another man to kill Dee Anna Justice. He was carrying a large sum of money that he admitted had been stolen from your grandmother, Bianca."

Bianca let out a relieved breath. "I never liked Roger."

"Me, either," Ester said. "He certainly pulled the wool over your grandmother's eyes for years."

"Where is your grandmother now?" Hud asked. "The police said they'd tried to reach her..."

Ester saw her alarm and quickly waved it off. "I got a text from my sister a few moments ago. May was looking after Marietta. She said the fool woman packed a bag and took the first flight out, headed this way."

There were surprised looks around the table. Then Dana got to her feet and announced, "I've made brunch. I think we should all have something to eat while we wait for our new arrival."

Hud said, "I'll have someone pick her up at the airport and bring her here. But the police in San Diego will still have a few questions for her."

DJ FELT AS IF she was in shock. She kept wanting to pinch herself. She'd gone from having only her father to having this family that kept getting bigger and bigger.

Dana told Bianca and Ester that they could stay in one of the cabins on the mountain as long as they wanted. "I know you and DJ have a lot to talk about. But first you have to share this brunch I've made."

"Are you sure there is enough?" Bianca asked. "We don't want to intrude."

Dana laughed. "I'm used to cooking for ranch hands. I always make too much. Anyway, you're fam-

ily. There is always room at my table for family." She
motioned DJ into the kitchen. "Are you all right?"

"I don't think I've ever been this all right," DJ
said, smiling. She felt exhausted from everything
that had happened. The Cardwells. Beau. Her near
death. And finally meeting her sister and the woman
who'd made her Trixie and had watched out for her
from a distance. It felt as if it was all too much. And
yet she'd never felt happier.

She hugged her cousin. "Thank you so much."

"It's just a little brunch," Dana said with a laugh.

"That and you, this ranch, everything you've
done. Somehow I feel as if it all had to come together here where it began."

"Have you heard how your father is doing?" Dana
asked.

"He's going to make it. His sentence is about up.
He's getting out of prison soon." DJ wasn't sure how
she felt about that. She could understand now why
he'd been afraid of her mother's family finding out
about her. The fact that he hadn't taken their money
made her almost proud of him. Maybe there was
more to her father than she'd originally thought.
Maybe when he got out they could spend some time
together, really get to know each other.

From the window, DJ could see Beau outside talking to Hud. Both looked worried. "They aren't going
to arrest my grandmother, are they?" DJ asked as
Dana followed her gaze to the two.

"No, I'm sure it is just as your sister said, a mistake, since that man has confessed to everything."

DJ hoped so. The marshal and Beau turned back toward the house. DJ stuck her head out the kitchen door to see Beau and Hud enter the house. Beau caught her eye and smiled reassuringly.

She felt a shaft of heat fall over her like the warm rays of the sun and almost blushed at the memory of their lovemaking. Beau was so tender and yet so strong and virile. Her heart beat a little faster just at the sight of him.

MARIETTA HAD ASSUMED she was being arrested when she landed at the airport and saw the two deputies waiting for her. She was pleasantly surprised to hear that she was being taken to the Cardwell Ranch, where her granddaughters were waiting for her.

On the drive up the canyon, she stared out at the snowy landscape, rough rocky cliffs and glazed-over green river. She'd never seen mountains like these, let alone this much snow, in her life. It kept her mind off what might be waiting for her once she reached the ranch.

Whatever was waiting, she deserved it, she told herself. She'd been a fool. The police had left a message that Roger Douglas had been arrested at the airport carrying a large amount of money on him. Her money. She shook her head. Who knew how much he had squandered? She would deal with that when she got home. If she got home.

Her chest ached. It was as if she could feel her old heart giving out. *Just stay with me a little longer. Let me try to fix this before I die.*

She was relieved when the deputy driving finally turned off the highway, crossed a bridge spanning the iced-over river and pulled down into a ranch yard. She stared at the large two-story house and took a breath. One of the deputies offered to help her out, but she waved him off.

This was something she had to do herself. It very well might be the last thing she ever did.

Chapter Nineteen

They had just sat down to eat Dana's brunch when they heard a patrol car drive up.

Everyone looked toward the front door expectantly. DJ wasn't sure she was ready to meet her grandmother. This was all happening too fast, and yet she couldn't help being curious. This was the woman who thankfully hadn't put a hit out on her. But she was the woman who'd apparently planned to buy her off.

Standing up, DJ prepared to meet her grandmother. Everyone else rose as well and moved into the living room. Hud went to open the door for the elderly woman who'd just climbed the steps and pounded forcibly on the door. She remembered Bianca saying the woman wasn't well, a bad heart. Now she wondered if that was true or if that was just what her grandmother wanted her to believe.

Like Beau, she hated always being suspicious. Wasn't there a chance that they could change? That love could make them more trusting?

Love? Where had that come from? She glanced over at Beau and felt her heart do that little jump it did when she saw him. She did love him.

The realization surprised her. She'd cared about some of the men she'd dated, but she'd never felt as if she was in love. Until this moment.

What a moment to realize it, she thought as an elderly woman with salt-and-pepper hair and intense brown eyes stepped into the room.

DJ felt Bianca take her hand. Beau was watching the older woman as if waiting for her to do something that would force him to take her down.

She almost laughed. He was so protective. He shot her a look that said, *You can do this.* She smiled. He had no idea how strange all this was for her. She'd dreamed of family, and now she had all the complications that came with one.

WHEN THE DOOR OPENED, Marietta almost fell in with it. "I want to see my granddaughter before you arrest me!" she said to the man in the marshal's uniform. It was just like them to have someone here to arrest her the moment she arrived at the house. But she wasn't leaving without a fight, she thought as the man stepped back and she barged in, more determined than ever.

What she saw made her stagger to a stop. Bianca standing next to a young woman who could have been her twin. Their resemblance to each other gave her a shock that almost stopped her old heart dead.

This was the child Carlotta had given birth to? This beautiful thing?

"What are you doing here?" Ester demanded. The accusation in her housekeeper's tone shocked her. Clearly their relationship had changed.

"You're starting to remind me of your sister," she snapped. "I came to see my granddaughter."

"*Which* granddaughter?" Bianca asked. She was holding DJ's hand, the two of them looking so formidable, so strong, so defiant. Her heart lodged in her throat as she looked at the two of them. She couldn't have been more proud or filled with shame. If she hadn't been the way she was, these two would have gotten to grow up together.

She could see her daughter in both of the women, but especially in DJ. The woman was more beautiful than even she knew. Marietta thought of that Bible verse about not hiding your light under a bushel basket. DJ was just coming into her own. Marietta wondered what had turned on that light inside her, then noticed the cowboy standing near her, looking just as fierce. Of course it had been a man.

"I came to see *both* granddaughters," she said and had to clear her voice. "But especially you, Dee Anna. I can't tell you how sorry I am that this is the first time we have ever met."

Carlotta was right. All she'd thought about was the family fortune and some ingrate of Walter Justice's trying to steal it. Staring at these two beautiful women, she felt a mountain of regret. She hadn't thought of Dee Anna as anything more than a mistake. She'd simply acted as she'd done all those years ago when she'd had Carlotta's marriage to Walter annulled. Both times she'd listened to Roger.

"DJ," Bianca said. "She goes by DJ."

Marietta smiled at her other granddaughter. She could see that the two women had already bonded. "DJ," she amended, her voice breaking as she held out her wrinkled hands to her granddaughter. "Can you ever forgive me?"

THERE WERE TEARS in her grandmother's eyes as DJ stepped to her and took both her hands in hers. Marietta pulled her into a hug. The older woman felt frail in her arms, and she was truly sorry that she hadn't known her before now.

"We should all sit down and have something to eat," Dana said. "Food and family go together."

"I need to ask Mrs. Pisani some questions," her marshal husband said.

"Not now. We are going to eat this brunch I made," Dana said in a no-nonsense tone as they gathered around the table again. "DJ, sit here by Beau and your grandmother. Ester and Bianca, would you mind sitting across from them? Hud—"

"Yep, I'm sitting down right where you tell me," he said.

A smattering of laughter moved through the room.

"I married a smart man," Dana said and introduced her husband and herself.

DJ didn't think she could eat a bite but was pleasantly surprised to find she could. "This is all so delicious," she told her cousin.

Everyone seemed to relax, commenting on how good the food was. Ester asked for one of the recipes. They talked about Montana, life on the ranch, Christmas and finally how they had come to know about each other. Marietta said little, picking at her food, her gaze on DJ.

Ester informed Marietta that Roger Douglas had been arrested. "He confessed not only to stealing your money but also to being behind hiring a hit man, so it looks like you're off the hook."

Her grandmother shook her head, smiling sadly. "We both know better than that. So much of this is my fault. Carlotta was right." She teared up again but quickly wiped her eyes. "I'm just so happy that my granddaughters have found each other."

WHEN THE MEAL was over, DJ was sorry to see it end. Dana had offered the cabins on the mountainside to Bianca, Ester and Marietta, but Bianca had declined, saying she was worried about her grandmother.

"She looks too pale," her sister had said confidentially to DJ. "She shouldn't have flown. I think all this might have been too much for her. I want to take her to the hospital to make sure she is all right."

"I'm not sure what good that will do," Ester said, not unkindly. "The doctors have told her there is nothing they can do for her. We've all known she doesn't have much longer."

"I know," Bianca said.

"Do you mind if I come with you to the hospital?" DJ asked.

"No, not at all," her sister said and smiled.

As Hud left to head back to work and they prepared to leave, snow began to fall as another storm came through. The clouds were low. So was the light. "I know you need this time with your family," Beau said as they all headed out onto the porch. "But if you need me…"

That was just it. She needed him too much. He crowded her thoughts and made her ache for the closeness they had shared.

"I'd like to finish helping you decorate the tree," she said.

"I'd like that, too. But we have time. Christmas is still days away."

"Yes," she said. "It's a date, then." She bit her tongue. "You know what I mean."

He nodded. "We kind of skipped that part. Maybe… well, depending on what you have planned after Christmas…"

They left it at that as he started toward his vehicle.

THE CRIME SCENE tape was gone. Everything seemed to be back to normal around Cardwell Ranch, Andrei thought as he watched the goings-on through the crosshairs of his rifle.

There'd been a lot of company today. He'd watched them come and go, the man with Dee Anna Justice giving her a little more space.

Several times he could have taken a shot, but it hadn't been perfect.

Now everyone seemed to be leaving. His birthday was only days away. He had to make his move. His leg was better. Good enough.

He adjusted the high-powered rifle and scope. It didn't take him long to get Dee Anna Justice in the crosshairs. A head shot was the most effective, but at this distance he didn't want to take the chance.

For days he'd been conflicted. But now he felt nothing but calm. His reputation was at stake. He would finish this.

Shooting into a crowd was always risky, but the confusion would give him his chance to make a clean getaway. Now it felt almost too easy. Was this the shot he'd been waiting for?

He aimed for DJ's heart and gently pulled the trigger.

DJ AND HER newfound family stood on the porch, saying their goodbyes to Dana. Her grandmother stood a few feet away. DJ heard Bianca ask her if she was feeling all right.

Beau had stopped near his pickup. She could feel his gaze on her. Something in his expression made her ache to be in this arms. He was dressed in jeans, boots and that red-and-black wool coat. His black Stetson was pulled low, but those blue eyes were on her. Her skin warmed at the thought of his hands on her.

"You're my granddaughter in every sense of the word," Marietta said as she stepped to DJ and took both of her hands again. "If I have any money left—"

"I don't want your money. I never have."

Her grandmother nodded. "I am such a foolish old woman."

DJ shook her head and hugged the woman. Marietta hugged her hard for a woman who looked so frail. As she stepped back, DJ heard Beau let out a curse.

She looked past her grandmother to see him running toward her. He was yelling, "Shooter! Everyone get down!"

DJ couldn't move, the words not making any sense at first. Then she reached for her grandmother. But Marietta pushed away her hand. As she looked up into the older woman's face, she found it filled with love and something else, a plea for forgiveness, in the instant before the woman stepped in front of her as if to shield her.

The next thing she knew, Beau slammed into her, knocking her to the porch floor. "Everyone down!"

In the distance came the roar of an engine. Beau was pushing her to move toward the door of the house. "Get inside! Hurry! DJ, are you hit?"

She couldn't do more than shake her head. "My grandmother?"

That's when she looked over and saw the woman lying beside her. Blood bloomed from her chest. DJ began to cry as Beau ushered them all inside the house, then carried Marietta in.

"Put her down here," Dana ordered, pointing to the couch near the Christmas tree. She had the phone in her hand. DJ knew she was already calling Hud and an ambulance.

She and her sister rushed to their grandmother's side.

"Stay here! No one leaves until I get back!" With that, Beau was gone.

Beau drew his own weapon from his shoulder holster. The sound of a vehicle engine turning over filled the icy winter air as he raced to his pickup. He could make out the silhouette of a vehicle roaring down the road toward Highway 191.

He started his engine, fishtailing as he punched the gas and went after it. By the time they reached the highway, he'd gained a little on what appeared to be an SUV.

The driver took off down the icy highway. Beau followed the two red taillights. He quickly got on his cell and called in the direction the man was headed, then tossed his cell aside to put all his attention on driving.

The highway was empty as the driver ahead of him left Big Sky behind and headed deeper into the canyon, going south toward West Yellowstone. But it was also icy. The last thing Beau wanted to do was end up in a ditch—or worse, the river. But he wasn't going to let the man get away.

As he raced after the vehicle, his mind raced, as well. Hud had been so sure that they had the hit man and that a local man had killed him. Was it possible another hit man had been hired when the first failed? Or had there always been two?

THIS WOULD BE how it ended. Andrei could see that now. For so long he'd had trouble envisioning his life after his forty-fifth birthday. Now he knew why.

He'd just killed some old woman. It was worse than he could have imagined. Shame made him burn. He had failed to kill his target and he wasn't going to get away, he thought as he looked back to see the pickup right behind him.

It was that cowboy. What was his story, anyway? The PI had been suspicious and jumpy from the start. Otherwise he wouldn't have spotted him just before he'd fired. The cowboy had probably caught the reflection off the rifle scope. Just Andrei's luck.

Ahead all he could see was snow. He hated snow. He hated cold. He hated this contract. All his instincts had told him to let it go. Stubbornness had made him determined to finish it no matter what. And all because of the coin toss. It had never let him down before. Not that it mattered now.

He felt his tires lose traction on the icy road. He touched his brakes as he felt the back of the car begin to slide and knew immediately that had been a mistake. But it was just another mistake, he thought as he cranked the wheel, trying to get the car to come out of the slide. Instead, it spun the other way. He was going too fast to save himself. He saw the guardrail coming up and closed his eyes.

BEAU'S HEART WAS POUNDING. He still couldn't believe how close DJ had come to being killed. If he hadn't lunged for her. If her grandmother hadn't stepped in front of the bullet. So many *if*s.

The taillights ahead of him grew brighter as he closed the distance. He knew this road. He suspected the would-be assassin did not. He could see that the vehicle was a white SUV. Probably a rental.

The canyon followed the river, winding through the mountains in tighter turns. He pressed harder, getting closer. His headlights shone into the vehicle, silhouetting the driver. A single male.

Just then, he saw that the driver had taken the curve too fast. He'd lost control. Beau watched the SUV go into a slide. He let up off his gas as best he could. He knew better than to hit his brakes. They would both end up in the river.

The SUV began a slow circle in the middle of the road. He could see that the driver was fighting like hell to keep it on the road, no doubt overcorrecting. The front of the SUV hit the guardrail and spun crazily toward the rock wall on the other side, where it crashed into the rocks, then shot back out, ping-ponging from the guardrail to the cliffs on the slick road until it finally came to rest against the rocks.

Beau managed to get stopped a few yards shy of the SUV. He turned on his flashers and jumped out, glad there wasn't any traffic. Drawing his weapon, he moved to the vehicle.

The driver was slumped to one side, his deflated air bag in his lap and blood smeared on what was left of the side window. Beau tried to open the driver's-side door, but it was too badly dented. He could hear sirens in the distance as he reached through the broken glass to put a finger to the man's throat. He was still breathing, but for how long?

"GRANDMAMA," BIANCA CRIED and fell to her knees beside the couch. DJ, taking the towel Dana handed her, pressed it to the bleeding wound in Marietta's chest.

"An ambulance is on the way," Dana assured her, sounding scared. The towel was quickly soaked with blood.

DJ joined her sister, her heart breaking. "You saved my life," she said to her grandmother. "Why would you do that?"

Marietta smiled through her pain. "It still can't make up for what I've done. If I had time…"

"You have time," Bianca said. "You can't leave us now."

Her grandmother patted her hand weakly. "My old heart was going to play out soon, anyway. I didn't want you to know how bad it was or how little time I had." She looked from Bianca to DJ and back. "Seeing the two of you together… I'm happy for you. You have a sister now."

She looked to DJ, reached for her hand and squeezed it. "Forgive me?" she whispered.

"Of course," DJ said, and her grandmother squeezed her fingers. "Take care of each other." Her gaze shifted to Ester. "Take care of my girls."

Ester nodded, tears in her eyes.

Marietta smiled and mouthed "Thank you" as her eyes slowly closed. Her hands went slack in theirs. She smiled then as if seeing someone she recognized on the other side.

Bianca began to cry. DJ put her arm around her, and the two hugged as the sound of sirens grew louder and louder.

Epilogue

Beau looked out his office window, watching the snowstorm and feeling restless. It was over. DJ was safe. The bad guys were either dead or in jail. It hadn't taken Marshal Hud Savage long to put all the pieces together with Beau's help. The man Roger Douglas had hired was arrested and quickly made a deal, naming not one but two hit men. Andrei Ivankov, a professional hit man, died before reaching the hospital in Bozeman. Jimmy Ryan, a thug for hire, was also dead, killed, according to lab results, by Ivankov.

Mailman Burt Olsen was in the clear. According to Dana, Burt and her sister, Stacy, had a date for New Year's. Dana figured they'd be planning a wedding by Valentine's Day. Apparently Stacy hadn't waited for Burt to ask her out. She'd invited him to the movies and they'd hit it off, making Dana say, "I told you so."

Meanwhile, Dana's best friend, Hilde, went into labor Christmas Eve. She had a beautiful eight-pound, nine-ounce baby boy. Dana had called earlier to ask if Beau had heard from DJ. He'd said he'd been busy and now wished he'd asked how DJ was doing, since he was sure Dana had talked to her.

"You going to spend the whole day looking out that window?" demanded a deep female voice behind him.

Beau turned to look guiltily at his assistant, Marge. She stood, hands on hips, giving him one of those looks. "What do you want me to do?"

"You should never have let her leave in the first place."

"She was going to her grandmother's funeral in Palm Desert."

"You could have gone along."

He shook his head. "She needed time."

Marge scoffed at that and shook her head as if disappointed in him. "You mean *you* needed time. Apparently you haven't had enough time in your life."

"I hardly know the woman."

Marge merely mugged a face at him.

"It was too soon," he said, turning back to the window. "She had too much going on right then." He glanced over his shoulder. Marge was gone, but she'd left the door open.

He walked out into the reception area of the office to find her standing at her desk. "What? You aren't going to keep nagging me?"

"Would it do any good?" She sounded sad. Almost as sad as he felt.

NEW YEAR'S DAY, Dana listened to the racket coming from her living room and smiled to herself. There were children laughing and playing, brothers arguing good-naturedly, sister and sisters-in-law talking food and fabrics, cousins discussing barbecue, since they had a batch of ribs going outside on the large grill. The house smelled of pine, fresh-brewed coffee and cocoa, and gingersnap cookies decorated by the children.

She wished her mother were here. How happy Mary Justice Cardwell would have been to see her family all together—finally. It was what Dana had hoped for all her life. It was one reason she would never leave this old house. Her children would grow up here—just as she had. She hoped that someday it would be her grandchildren she would hear playing in the next room.

"Do you need any help?" her cousin DJ asked from the kitchen doorway.

Dana stepped to her and pulled her into a hug. "Having you here means more than you can ever know." She drew back to look at her cousin. She'd seen how much Beau and DJ had loved each other. But for whatever reason, they'd parted. It broke her heart.

She'd had to twist DJ's arm to get her to fly up for the New Year. "You wouldn't consider staying longer, would you?"

"I have to return to California. My editor has a list of assignments she wants me to consider."

"I have to ask about your grandmother's funeral," Dana said.

"It was quite beautiful. As misguided as she was in the past, she saved my life. I'll never forget that. Also, I've been spending time with my sister and my father, actually. He's trying to figure out what he wants to do with the rest of his life. That was nice of you to offer him a place here on the ranch."

"I hope he takes me up on it," Dana said. "After all, this is where he belongs. Zinnia would love to see him again. You know, she's a widow."

DJ laughed. "You just can't help matchmaking, can you?"

"I have no idea what you're talking about," Dana said, smiling. "Bianca is also always welcome here on the ranch. I spoke with her about coming up and spending a few weeks. She wants to learn to ride horses. So you have to come back. There really is no place like Montana in the summer."

"You sound like Beau." DJ seemed to catch herself. "He mentioned how nice it is up here once the snow melts."

"Yes, Beau," Dana said, unable to hold back a grin. "The night I saw the two of you dancing down at The Corral, I knew you were perfect for each other."

DJ shook her head. "I'm afraid you're wrong about that. I haven't heard from him since I left."

Dana laughed. "Trust me. I'm never wrong."

IT WAS ALMOST midnight when there was a knock at the door. The old ranch house on Cardwell Ranch was full of family. Dana had just passed out the noisemakers. DJ had seen her watching the door as if she was expecting more guests, but everyone was already there, including DJ's cousins—Jordan and his wife, Stacy and Burt, and even Clay and his partner.

Dana ran to the door and threw it open. A gust of cold air rushed in. DJ saw her cousin reach out, grab Beau and pull him in. They shared a few words before both looked in her direction.

She groaned, afraid of what Dana had done to get Beau over here tonight. Her cousin was so certain she wasn't wrong making this match. DJ almost felt sorry for her. As much as she and Beau had enjoyed their time together, as much as DJ felt for him, sometimes things just didn't work out, she told herself as he walked toward her.

If anything, he was more handsome than the first time she'd seen him standing in the airport. His blue eyes were on her, and in them she saw what almost looked like pain. Her heart lodged in her throat. Tears burned her eyes.

"We need to talk," he said as he took her hand. She was reminded of the night at The Corral when he'd said the same words. Only that night, he'd dragged her from the dance floor, out into the snowy night.

Tonight he led her into the kitchen and closed the door. When he turned to her, she looked into his handsome face and felt her pulse pound.

"I'm a damned fool," he said. "I should never have let you go. Or at least, I should have gone with you. Since the day you left, I've thought about nothing but you. I would have called, but I was afraid that once you got back to your life…"

"Are you just going to talk, or are you going to kiss me?" DJ managed to say, her heart in her throat.

He pulled her to him. His mouth dropped to hers. He smelled of snow and pine and male. She breathed him in as he deepened the kiss and held her tighter.

"I never want to let you go," he said when he drew back. "If that means leaving Montana—"

"I would never ask you to leave a place you love so much."

He looked into her eyes. "Then what are we going to do? Because I don't want to spend another day without you."

"With my job, I can work anywhere."

He smiled, his blue eyes sparkling. "You'd move to Montana if I were to…ask you?"

"What are you saying, cowboy?"

He looked down at his boots for a moment, then met her gaze again. "I never saw you coming. This was the last thing I expected, but now that you've come into my life… Come back. Come back to me. I know it probably seems like we haven't known each other that long, but…" His hand went into his pocket. He seemed to hesitate as he studied her face for a moment.

DJ held her breath as he pulled his hand from his pocket and opened it. Sitting in the middle of his large palm, something caught the light.

She felt her eyes widen at the sight of the diamond ring lying there.

"It was my mother's. She left it with her sister so my father didn't pawn it."

DJ couldn't help but smile knowingly. She and Beau. Their connection, as odd as it was, ran deep.

"Would you consider marrying me? Not right away. We could have as long an engagement as you need." He seemed to catch himself and dropped to one knee. "I know this should have been more romantic—"

She shook her head. "It's perfect," she said, seeing his discomfort. She held out her left hand. "And yes, I will marry you. And no, I don't need a long engagement. Leaving here, leaving you, was one of the hardest things I've ever done. It was breaking my heart." Her eyes filled with tears. "Montana feels like the home I've never had. Somehow, I've never felt that I deserved to be happy. But with you…"

He slipped the ring on her finger, rose and pulled her into his arms. "That's exactly how I feel. As if

I deserve this if I'm smart enough not to let you get away."

She smiled as he lowered his mouth to hers. "I love you, DJ," he whispered against her lips. In the next room, a cheer arose. It was a new day, a new year.

* * * * *

COMING NEXT MONTH FROM

H HARLEQUIN®
™

I N T R I G U E

Available December 20, 2016

#1683 RIDING SHOTGUN
The Kavanaughs • by Joanna Wayne
Pierce Lawrence returns to the Double K ranch a war hero after two tours as a SEAL ready to bond with his five-year-old daughter. Grace Cotton has been on the run from her ex in witness protection, but maybe Pierce and his daughter are the homecoming she's been waiting for.

#1684 ONE TOUGH TEXAN
Cattlemen Crime Club • by Barb Han
Alice Green, a young cop, goes rogue to save a young girl after she believes her actions led to the girl's abduction. Joshua O'Brien knows a thing or two about putting everything on the line. But can Alice open up enough to let the handsome rancher aid in her mission?

#1685 TURQUOISE GUARDIAN
Apache Protectors: Tribal Thunder • by Jenna Kernan
Apache guardian Carter Bear Den rescues his former fiancée, Amber Kitcheyan, from a mass shooting at the hands of an eco-extremist. But Amber is the only living witness—and what she knows might get them both killed.

#1686 BATTLE TESTED
Omega Sector: Critical Response • by Janie Crouch
Rosalyn Mellinger never meant to dupe Steve Drackett, head of the Critical Response Division of Omega Sector—she fled after their weekend of passion to protect him from her ruthless stalker, The Watcher. But now Steve is the only one who can protect her...and their unborn child.

#1687 STONE COLD TEXAS RANGER
by Nicole Helm
Vaughn Cooper is a by-the-book Texas Ranger. Natalie Torres is a hypnotist brought in to crack the witness in an ongoing investigation. It's distrust at first sight, but only together can they withstand the coming danger.

#1688 SAN ANTONIO SECRET
by Robin Perini
When Sierra Bradford's best friend and goddaughter are abducted, she vows to find them at any cost. Even if that means teaming up with former Green Beret Rafe Vargas, who's come to her aid...and not for the first time.

YOU CAN FIND MORE INFORMATION ON UPCOMING HARLEQUIN® TITLES, FREE EXCERPTS AND MORE AT WWW.HARLEQUIN.COM.

HICNM1216

SPECIAL EXCERPT FROM

*A popular girl goes missing, and everyone
close to her has something to hide.*

*Go inside the mind of a criminal in the fourth book in
the riveting **THE PROFILER** series:
STALKED by Elizabeth Heiter.*

"Where are you, Haley?" Linda whispered into the
stillness of her daughter's room.

Today marked exactly a month since her daughter
had gone missing. Since Haley's boyfriend, Jordan, had
dropped her off at school for cheerleading practice. Since
her best friend Marissa had waved to her from the field
on that unusually warm day, watched her walk into the
school, presumably to change before joining Marissa at
practice.

She'd never walked out again.

How did a teenage girl go missing from *inside* her
high school? No one could answer that for Linda. As time
went by, they seemed to have fewer answers and more
questions.

But Linda *knew*—with some deep part of her she
could only explain as mother's intuition—that Haley was
out there somewhere. Not buried in an unmarked grave,
as she'd overheard two cops speculating when day after
day passed with no more clues. Haley was still alive, and
just waiting for someone to bring her home.

Linda clutched Haley's bright pink sweatshirt tighter. She fell against the bed, trying to hold her sobs in, and the mattress slid away from her, away from the box spring.

Linda froze as the edge of a tiny black notebook caught her attention.

The book was jammed between the box spring and the bed frame. The police must have missed it, because she'd seen them peer underneath Haley's mattress when they'd looked through the room, assessing her daughter's things so matter-of-factly.

Linda's pulse skyrocketed as she yanked it out. She didn't recognize the notebook, but when she opened the cover, there was no mistaking her daughter's girlie handwriting. And the words…

She dropped the notebook, practically flung it away from her in her desire to get rid of it, to unsee it. She didn't realize she'd started screaming until her husband ran into the room and wrapped his arms around her.

"What? What is it?" he kept asking, but all she could do was sob and point a shaking hand at the notebook, lying open to the first page, and Haley's distinctive scrawl:

If you're reading this, I'm already dead.

Follow FBI profiler Evelyn Baine as she tries to uncover which of Haley's secrets might have led to her disappearance.

STALKED
by Elizabeth Heiter
Available December 27, 2016,
from MIRA Books.

$1.⁰⁰ OFF

ELIZABETH HEITER

Secrets can be deadly...

STALKED

MIRA®

Available December 27, 2016

Order your copy today!

$7.99 U.S./$9.99 CAN.

$1.⁰⁰ OFF the purchase price of STALKED by Elizabeth Heiter.

Offer valid from December 17, 2016, to June 17, 2017.
Redeemable at participating retail outlets, in-store only. Not redeemable at
Barnes & Noble. Limit one coupon per purchase. Valid in the U.S.A. and Canada only.

52614428

Canadian Retailers: Harlequin Enterprises Limited will pay the face value of this coupon plus 10.25¢ if submitted by customer for this product only. Any other use constitutes fraud. Coupon is nonassignable. Void if taxed, prohibited or restricted by law. Consumer must pay any government taxes. Void if copied. Inmar Promotional Services ("IPS") customers submit coupons and proof of sales to Harlequin Enterprises Limited, P.O. Box 3000, Saint John, NB E2L 4L3, Canada. Non-IPS retailer—for reimbursement submit coupons and proof of sales directly to Harlequin Enterprises Limited, Retail Marketing Department, 225 Duncan Mill Rd., Don Mills, ON M3B 3K9, Canada.

U.S. Retailers: Harlequin Enterprises Limited will pay the face value of this coupon plus 8¢ if submitted by customer for this product only. Any other use constitutes fraud. Coupon is nonassignable. Void if taxed, prohibited or restricted by law. Consumer must pay any government taxes. Void if copied. For reimbursement submit coupons and proof of sales directly to Harlequin Enterprises, Ltd 482, NCH Marketing Services, P.O. Box 880001, El Paso, TX 88588-0001, U.S.A. Cash value 1/100 cents.

5 65373 00076 2 (8100)0 12233

® and ™ are trademarks owned and used by the trademark owner and/or its licensee.

© 2016 Harlequin Enterprises Limited

MCOUPEH1216

THE WORLD IS BETTER WITH

Romance

Harlequin has everything from contemporary, passionate and heartwarming to suspenseful and inspirational stories.

Whatever your mood, we have a romance just for you!

Connect with us to find your next great read, special offers and more.